Tombstone Tea

TOMBSTONE TEA

JOANNE DAHME

RP TEENS
PHILADELPHIA · LONDON

Library of Congress Control Number: 2009924760

ISBN 978-0-7624-3718-4

Cover illustration by Frank Sipala
Cover and interior design by Frances J. Soo Ping Chow
Edited by Kelli Chipponeri
Typography: Bembo, Caslon 540, and Type Embellishments

Running Press Teens is an imprint of
Running Press Book Publishers
2300 Chestnut Street
Philadelphia, PA 19103-4371

Visit us on the web!
www.runningpress.com

To

My husband, Joe and my son, Will

My nieces and nephews: Jennifer, Liam, and Paddy

My lifelong friends: Brigid, Cathy, Gina,
Joan, and Meredith

———◆———

*Thanks for sharing my life's adventures
(and love of cemeteries)*

I CAN'T SEEM TO TOUCH HER...

PROLOGUE

I can see them, through the blur and the haze of the night, despite their efforts to blind my vision with spirit light.

I'm not that far. They know I am lurking in the shadows of the crypts, in the cool morning dew on the grass, in the white, peeling bark of the sycamore trees. Nature, unlike the spirits, cannot deny my presence here.

I want my daughter. Why does that provoke such hysterical activity among the dead? Who are these things to separate us, to keep us apart from each other? She is my daughter and I am her mother and I'll be damned if they succeed in keeping her from me.

How long has it been since I lost her? My daughter's death carries the weight of a century.

How long have I been screaming her name? Long enough that the sound of "Amy" implored across the heavens has merged with the caw of the birds and the roar of the wind as it blusters through the fully dressed trees. Nature has taken the name, as it does all names cried across the millennium, and has cocooned it beneath its own clamoring.

She has never answered me. Surely there has been some interference.

And I can't seem to touch her grave, despite the walls of my own coffin sharing the same vein of compacted soil.

What are they doing there, amid the glowing hysteria of the dithering spirits of Laurel Hill? They are lighting their candles against the darkness. Am I the darkness that causes them to tremble? Perhaps they know that I will ravage them if they try to stop me. Tonight is the night that I will reclaim my daughter.

Ahhh. I can see them. Elisha, Adam, and Paul—three fools who cannot let go of this world, for no other reason beyond their sentimental attachment to it. Elisha, the feckless leader. Paul, the naive child. Adam, the feeble-minded clown. The spirits are in dire need of some capable leadership.

But the girl. Her life force is strong. I have followed it each time she has passed through the cemetery's gates. During the last cool season, when the leaves were dying all around us, I was almost able to claim her, to use her gift, much as I tried to use Paul's so long ago, to reunite with my Amy.

But what do they do? They are walking as one through the cemetery now, the girl and her three ridiculous ghosts in tow. One would think they were a traveling carnival, what with the bursts of light rising above the mausoleums and other grand tombs like cheap fireworks. They wish to distract me and to blind me to their destination.

Even the birds and other creatures are restless, moving about the landscape as if they were running from a roaring fire. They are always the first to sense a change in the natural forces. Perhaps the supernatural ones hold similar sway.

Dare they ridicule me? Do they think that I cannot see where they are going and to what end they hope to prod the girl? Those foolish women are waiting for them. Stupid women who believe that they can cast some light on another's shadowed world.

Do they think that we're some Tombstone Tea, our garden chairs arranged around the grave of a favorite uncle, sharing fond memories of his antics as we sip from our china cups? But our tea is as tepid as our presence here, as the spirits outnumber the living too many tombs to one. It is time to end this party.

SATURDAY,
the 30th day of September,
at 10 p.m.

A TOMBSTONE TEA

AT LAUREL HILL CEMETERY
Tickets for Sale at the Entrance House

The Dare

O n a late September Friday after school, most girls my age would be looking forward to a trip to the mall, a movie, or maybe even a date. Not me. There I was, my back pressed against the rough white stone of just one of the thousands of obelisks that could be found in the Laurel Hill Cemetery. Was I feeling sorry for myself? Maybe. If only I could have ignored the turbulence in my stomach and the wiggle in my knees. Spending the night alone in a cemetery searching for ten special gravestones was not bringing out the best in me.

I was new to Philadelphia and, worse yet, a sophomore at the Laurel Hill Charter High School that, despite its only being around for one full year, was already packed with clubs and cliques and gangs that were hard to break into. My high school in Doylestown was not much different in that sense, but at least I had established an identity for myself there that included friends.

When you grow up in one place, you have a core group of kids who have known you since preschool or kindergarten. That's how it was for me in high school. My closest friends, and even many of the kids that I just passed in the hallway or shared classes with, were used to me being a little *different*. I zone out sometimes and it seemed to happen a lot at my high school in Doylestown, which was built more than one hundred years ago. Sometimes, right in the middle of a class discussion, I'd get a sense of other kids who weren't physically in the room. A face would flash before my eyes, or I'd hear a voice I did not recognize whisper or laugh in my ear. It was a bit distracting and, of course, I never shared this with anyone. People would think that I was crazy, although it had happened in small ways for as long as I could remember, particularly if I was in a place that had some history. But I got the reputation of having some kind of attention disorder. My friends liked to say that I was taking a *time-out* from reality. *Jessie is timing out,* they would laugh. That usually brought me back.

Despite this quirk of mine, I had been a starter on the lacrosse team, played flute in the band, and was in first track. But when we moved into our East Falls neighborhood in August, I knew that the panic that started squeezing my lungs was legit, and for good reason. I was really nervous about making new friends. How would they react to my *dropping out* periodically? I did not want people thinking I was a head case. And if I was not feeling neurotic enough, I found out that my new school was an *experimental* one.

Experimental, I had echoed, when my parents unloaded that one on me, lacing my voice with as much contempt as I could muster. Dad beamed his brightest smile just to irritate me. In his view of the world, I should have been thrilled to learn that my new school had partnered with the oldest private cemetery in the country to focus a "history-structured" curriculum. Dad was an aging hippie who was recently hired by the Philadelphia School District to make "Philadelphia schools more like the subur-ban schools." Those are *his* words. And sending his only child—I substituted *sacrificing* in my head—to the charter school was part of the job.

"City students should be offered innovative and challenging curriculums to better engage them in the world, just as their suburban counterparts," he shared with me recently over breakfast. He was resting both elbows on the kitchen table and leaning in toward me in that over animated position he assumes when he's excited about something. His blond white hair looked as it did when he got out of bed and his black-framed glasses reflected a smudge or two. This is what happens when Dad is engrossed by something. He forgets all about his personal appearance. I'm glad I did not inherit that quirk.

"Laurel Hill Cemetery was established in 1836, Jessie, at a time when church graveyards were running out of space as Philadelphia was growing. Victorians, who lived in the nineteenth century, craved to get away from the city during the heat of summer and also thought it was really important to remember their dead. As a result, the cemetery became this magnificent outdoor sculpture garden, the more elaborate the better." Dad finally paused to take a breath.

"It's a cemetery, Dad," I tried to deadpan to kill his enthusiasm. "Nothing but dead people." I attempted to focus on cutting the crust from my toast.

He waved my statement away with his hand. "It is art, it is nature, and it is Philadelphia's history, all wrapped up in eighty acres of hills and cliffs that overlook the Schuylkill River."

"Did the cemetery give you a job, too?" I asked, doing my best to sound peevish. His enthusiasm was hard to torpedo. And it wasn't just his enthusiasm that was annoying me. I was getting nervous about how *old* the place was, because of my timing out predilection.

He flashed me what Mom calls his salesman smile as he reached out to tussle my hair. "You are going to love it, Jessie. Just give it a chance."

I rewarded him with a fake smile because I was still pretty miserable about the whole thing. It was bad enough going to a new high school, but did it have to be *this* one? I don't like history, I don't like cemeteries, and the fact that the high school was in an old Pep Boys building—the posters of Manny, Moe, and Jack are still plastered all over the school to remind us of *its* history—provided enough clues to tell me that this was a lousy match. And what was even more bizarre was the neighborhood. We were living on Midvale Avenue, where there are blocks and blocks of large stone houses with really big yards. But the charter school, which was only about a half mile away, was in a row-house neighborhood that obviously had seen better days. And even though the school population was pretty diverse, sometimes when I was getting on and off the SEPTA bus, I noticed the African-American residents looking at us warily. I was an outsider two times over.

That's why, when Michelle approached me in the hall between math and English periods that Monday to ask if

I was interested in joining her *group*, I was in such a weakened and desperate state that I would have signed up to sell candy for the *Robotics* Club.

It had sounded so simple when Michelle, Jeanne, and Melanie surrounded me after school to tell me what I was to do.

"It's easy, Jessie," Michelle sniffed. "We all did it." But the way they looked at one another with their upturned noses and snarky smiles made me doubt it.

"Here's the deal," she continued, her mascaraed blue eyes suddenly looking solemn. "We'll drop you off at seven o'clock at the cemetery—Jeanne can drive," she added, seeing my raised eyebrows. "We'll give you a list of the ten graves you have to find during the night, and to prove you found them," she built up momentously, "you need to make rubbings of each stone."

"Rubbings?" I echoed. "Like we did in grade school of fossils and things?"

"Yes, rubbings," Melanie repeated, seemingly anxious to get a word in between her bubble-gum blowing.

I should have paid attention to the nervous leaps my stomach made. The girls standing in front of me were blond by varying degrees, the kind of blonds that toss their long, flowing hair across their shoulders when looking bored. They were all cute, too, in that fair sort of way—blue eyes, turned-up noses, sexy smiles. They dressed in skinny jeans and halters, with hobo bags slung over their shoulders, and multiple piercings in their ears. I have short brown hair, green eyes, and my face, like the rest of my body, is covered in freckles. And I'm afraid of piercings. I should have known better as they were being so nice to me, inviting me to become one of them, despite my lack of blondness.

"But why the cemetery?" I asked, without saying out loud that this group did not look like the student booster type that embraced everything their school symbolized without question. Michelle usually looked catatonic in history class.

Michelle's eyes got wider than she normally worked them. "Last year, we all spent a night in the cemetery. But since you're new, you'll need to do it alone. It's a tradition!" she insisted. "Besides, it's really cool, just like in the movies."

I wanted to say people usually die in the movies when hanging out in cemeteries, especially when they are alone. The three of them nodded encouragingly on cue. And because I wanted to please them and was desperate to feel like a part of the group, I agreed to meet them after school on Friday with a backpack filled with a few snacks, a flashlight, some crayons, and paper. Could my school's adopted cemetery really be that bad?

———◦◉◦———

What if I die here? I worried, as the evening's shadows slowly began descending across the faces of the tombstones and obelisks that jutted jauntily from the plunging hillside. I had told my mother that I was sleeping over at Melanie's house. I would hate to be found dead the day after I lied to my mother. She doesn't appreciate that kind of thing.

I took a deep breath and inhaled the hay like smell of grass and the mud-tinged breeze rising from the Schuylkill River, which rushed invisible to me now at the foot of the cemetery hillside, furiously swollen still from a late summer rain. I was standing in a small asphalt parking lot on Ridge Avenue across the street from the cemetery's entrance. The girls were giddy when they pulled into the lot, seemingly anxious to unload me in case I changed my mind. Their laughter gnawed at my quickly fraying trust of their good intentions.

"Give her the map," Jeanne screeched as Melanie rolled down the car window to toss it into the wind before they pulled away.

I snatched at the map, praying that it would say something like "Joke's on you!" or "September's Fool!" although that would have been lame, but I wouldn't have cared. Instead it showed the cemetery entrance, which was looming across the street in front of me. Even more unnerving, the map showed what looked to be miles of pathways that wove around numbered or lettered sections of the cemetery. The cemetery was divided into "North," "Central," and "South," and only the Schuylkill River stopped it from spreading its tombstones further.

The Entrance House, as it was labeled on the map, looked as if it had traveled through a time portal. It, and the sprawling green acreage behind its combination of chain-linked and spike–tipped black iron fencing, stared back at a world of asphalt streets, scuffed brick row houses that teetered close to the sidewalk curbs, and large, windowless brick hulks of long-gone industries, their dormant smokestacks still reaching for the sky.

The Entrance House was shielded by a row of cream-colored wooden columns. Oddly enough, it reminded me of a southern mansion whose owners had the misfortunate impulse to add living quarters on both sides. The windows, in both the columned portion of the building and its wings, looked relatively new and were curtained, as if still occupied. What was unique about the Entrance House itself was the gaping hole right through its center that accommodated the cobblestoned driveway that sucked cars through its arch. A thick black wrought-iron gate barred the entrance to the driveway now, but instead of protecting crops of cotton or tobacco as it would have done on a southern plantation, the gate was busy keeping the living neighbors away from the quieter, dead ones.

From this vantage point, I had a view of the cemetery that could have been breathtaking—if I *liked* cemeteries. But the fact was, I had never seen a cemetery so crowded with gravestones of all sorts and sizes, headstone to head-stone like these were. Even the scary-looking mausoleums were lined up like Philadelphia row houses—a regular neighborhood of ghosts. How would I ever find the ten graves that the girls had chosen, without the help of . . . I didn't want to even think about it. If old schools like my high school in Doylestown distracted me with a flash of images of people I didn't know, what effect would a cemetery have on me? Now was not the moment to time out.

The entrance gate was locked, of course, so I squeezed through the space between the gates that were held closed with a chain that was just long enough to let me pass.

I ran quickly beneath the arch without looking back, following the curve of the path. As my focus was on my feet, I nearly stumbled face-first into a towering obelisk that leaned slightly toward a neighboring pedestal with a black iron angel perched upon it. The angel's outstretched hand could touch my shoulder if I only leaned a bit closer.

I huddled against the angel, whose metal curly locks and little-girl face gave it a cherubic look, as the cemetery shadows swallowed up the neighborhood. I tried to slow my breathing as my lungs filled with old air. *Old air,* I mocked myself. That is utterly ridiculous. As if the cemetery's air was petrified like an ancient bug caught in amber. I wasn't frozen in time here. I could just dash through those gates and run as fast as I could, past those houses, past my school, into my tree-filled East Falls neighborhood.

But I wouldn't do that. I needed friends. Needed them badly enough that I was willing to spend a long night with sweaty palms and a thumping heart. I glanced at the angel's face and for a moment felt as if she were really looking at me, almost as if she were tilting her head to get a read on my situation. I looked at the tombstone she hovered over.

AMY HALPRIN
Dear Daughter of Jenny and Robert
1889–1906

Seventeen. Just a year older than me. I shivered because, of course, cemeteries are not just for old people. I reached into my backpack and took a good gulp of water. Then I poured a little bit on my hands and sprinkled myself with a few drops of the bottled product—an on-the-spot baptism. Superstitions aren't rational.

I tugged my sweatshirt sleeves down to my wrists. My back felt cool against the stone of the obelisk, and the gauzy light cast by the just-rising full moon seemed to gently blanket whatever gesture of heat the early fall day had lent to the earth. *Full moon,* I realized as I caught my breath. In movies, full moons were prime time for werewolves and other shape-shifters that lived in the woods. If that were the case, I would rather be in a ghostly glowing cemetery than stumbling around in a dark forest into who knows what. Cemeteries were civilized. The grass was cut and gravestones were placed in neat rows. The illumination of moonlight should help in locating the assigned tombstones, too.

Tombstones, I reminded myself. I couldn't sit here all night, I thought as I forced myself to stand by pushing my back against the rough face of the obelisk. Maybe if I really focused I could finish the job in a few hours. I could tell my mom that I started feeling a little homesick and decided to leave Melanie's before the girls went to bed.

I gasped at the sound of approaching footsteps. Strolling around the bend of the cobblestoned cemetery driveway was a guy.

"Hey there!" he called, waving in my direction. *Run!* my mind commanded, but my feet were bolted to the ground. He began jogging toward me. The force of my pounding heart nearly knocked me over. I tried to remember what they taught us in school about self defense. Nothing came to my scrambled mind.

He stood in front of me within seconds. Did he really run that fast, I marveled. His face was smooth, hair shaggy, eyes silver in the graying dusk, and his skin glowed in the moonlight. He wore ill-fitting jeans and a dirty flannel shirt with sleeves rolled up to his elbows. His bare arms showed tiny little scar-like scratches that had been sunburned into permanence.

"Why are you staring at me like that?" he accused, cocking his head. I suddenly smelled evergreen trees as he spoke. "You're the trespasser, not me, you know," he added sternly, in a voice that sounded older than his body. "If you didn't have all those freckles spritzed across your face, I'd be calling the police." This time he smiled, a kind, joking smile.

"I'm sorry. I didn't mean to stare at you," I stammered, between beats of my hammering heart. I glanced around for an escape route, taking a nervous step back. "It's just that you . . . surprised me," I added lamely. I jumped as Amy's angel touched my back. *Amy.* The thought flickered through my mind, as if I knew her.

"Forgive me. I sacred you, didn't I?" He gave me that reassuring smile again. "I work here. You don't have any spray paint or anything in your backpack, do you?"

"Spray paint?" I echoed, clueless. I thought of the cemeteries back in Doylestown, where the high school kids hung out drinking or smoking. I'd seen plenty of beer cans in the cemeteries I cut through with friends but never any spray paint cans.

"Kids sometimes get in here and tag the tombstones. You know, graffiti them up. It's my job to make sure that that doesn't happen."

"Oh, no. I don't have any spray paint," I replied, maybe a bit too quickly. I shifted the weight of my backpack guiltily, thinking of that pack of crayons.

"Then what *are* you doing here?" he asked, taking another step closer and invading my personal space.

For a panicked second, I felt a fluttering, like the wings of a large bird brushing against my back. The air suddenly seemed to fill with hot, urgent whisperings. I swung around, to see nothing but the shadowed forms of graveyard statues, stones, and obelisks prickling the cemetery landscape. The iron angel peered down at me sympathetically. *Stop it,* I pleaded with myself. *Don't time out now in front of this stranger.*

He touched my arm and I jumped at the coolness of his fingers. "Are you all right?" he asked, his forehead now scrunched with concern.

I didn't know what to say. I didn't know what to make of this feeling that I was getting—a thousand hands anxiously touching me. *This* never happened at my Doylestown High School. I'd never physically felt a presence.

From my obelisk, for it was *my* obelisk now as I hadn't torn away from it since I barreled into the cemetery, I could see the battered houses across the street as he no longer blocked that path. I saw shadows of kids playing in the street. I could hear music blaring from the thumping speakers in someone's living room. And yet, standing here, on the other side of the black iron fence, I felt as if I was disconnected from the real world. *Can a cemetery gate truly divide the living from the dead?*

"I'm okay," I replied quickly, wishing to brush him off. "You really work here?" I repeated. "In the cemetery? At night?" I ran my hands over my arms, the way one does when brushing off invisible spiderwebs. My imagination was getting the best of me. *He works here, he works here*, I kept repeating to myself.

"Well, yes. It's not that odd." He squinted as if annoyed. "I work on weekends. I'm sort of like a night watchman. Just wander around to make sure that everything is all right here, like I just said. It's not like it used to be, you know. People don't always respect the cemetery."

A soft breeze suddenly blew from the ground. I felt its warm fingers caressing my cheeks and hair. It smelled tangy, like burning leaves. I looked around at the cemetery's army of sculptures. I could not imagine anyone coming in here and not feeling menaced by their suggested power in the darkness.

"What's your name?" I asked, needing to make him human.

"Paul," he replied, standing straighter. "Who are you?" he shot back.

"My name is Jessie," I said. "You only work on weekends?" I pressed. He couldn't be much older than me.

"Yeah, that's when all the trouble occurs. Kids like to

spook each other and make dares."

Like my dare, I thought. But at least I wasn't here to hurt anything.

"I like it here," he continued. "It's quiet, but never lonely."

I'm sure my eyebrows were raised. My mom tells me it is a curse that I cannot hide my skepticism about anything.

"Do you have family here?" I asked, offering him an explanation.

"Family?" he repeated thoughtfully and then paused. "I guess you could say that."

That was *not* the kind of answer I wanted to hear. I looked longingly at the gate.

"Do you have any ID?" I blurted, almost embarrassed.

Paul laughed. "Hey, I should be asking you that. You're the one who's trespassing."

"I do have my school ID," I said, patting my backpack, where it would stay.

Paul nodded, but didn't press for my card. "Here," he said, pulling a card from the front pocket of his flannel shirt. "It's a little beat up, so it might be hard to read."

His movement released a smell like attic air. *Would everything in the cemetery start smelling like that after a little while?* I wondered.

I took the card, which felt warm despite the chilly air.

The card was made from thick paper, but a lot of the stuff on it was blotted out by mold. The photograph showed somebody about Paul's age with dark hair, but it was hard to say exactly that it was Paul. I could make out *Laurel Hill Cemetery* at the top of the card.

"I've lost it a few times on the grounds. Sometimes it's weeks before one of the maintenance guys finds it." He shrugged when I handed it back. He slipped it into his shirt pocket. "When I clean it up, it looks exactly like me."

"Can't they give you a new card?" I asked. If I were going to make it through this night, I realized that I needed Paul to be who he claimed to be. Alone, my imagination might reduce me to a white-haired lunatic by morning. I wanted so badly to trust him.

He tilted his head at me as if it were a novel thought. "You know, I never worried about it. I never use it since everyone who works here knows me. I guess I never thought that a trespasser would demand it of me."

I think I actually tilted my head in response. It sounded reasonable.

"So what are *you* doing here tonight, Jessie?" He glanced around the cemetery as if he noticed someone was listening. His gaze darted back to mine. "You're the one that should be explaining to me," he said, standing straight and resting his hands on his hips like an adult.

"Well, it's a long story," I told him, "so I will attempt to tell the very short version." I shifted the weight of my backpack on my shoulder as if it bore the weight of the longer tale. "I am new in Philadelphia and am a sophomore at the Laurel Hill Charter High School."

Paul beamed at the name. "Why don't they call it Laurel Hill *Cemetery* Charter High School? Isn't that what they mean?" he asked with all sincerity.

"Because it is a *school*," I snapped a bit too quickly. This is always what happens when I am on edge. I attempted a polite smile. "Anyway, these girls in my class kind of dared me to spend the night in the cemetery to track down some gravestones to get rubbings. Kind of like a fraternity hazing," I added hopefully, wishing so badly that it were so.

"Did that scare you?" he asked quietly.

I didn't want to say that I was petrified at the thought. I shook my head. "I was—am—afraid that I won't be able to find all the tombstones."

"Well, I know every grave in the cemetery. I can help you track them down," he promised, a little too enthusiastically. He made a sweeping motion with his arm. "I bet there isn't a grave I can't find. And," he added, "you're in luck tonight."

Was the world suddenly holding its breath? The crickets and owls went quiet, as if to allow unseen ears to hear. The sycamore tree behind us thrilled as the wind combed its leaves. *By the pricking of my thumbs,* I thought, having just tackled my Shakespeare reading assignment. I wondered if a cemetery had given him inspiration.

"Really?" I replied, just a little doubtful. "Did I win something?" I asked stupidly. If I ran now, would he be caught off guard?

He grinned. *At me or someone over my head?* I looked into the grasping branches of the sycamore. No one was there, but my eyes couldn't help registering the hundreds of solid, shadowed gravestones that fanned across the hilly landscape, packing the grassy terraces that rose to the rim of the horizon, between the winding asphalt driveway and smaller walking paths. Trees bent protectively over their stone charges. The air smelled of dirt, newly shoveled.

"Yeah," he answered excitedly. "When I first spotted you, I thought you might be here a day early for the Tombstone Tea!" He paused, as if he wanted the weight of his pronouncement to properly sink in.

"Tombstone Tea?" I echoed weakly. "Do you mean there's going to be a party in the *cemetery*?" Things were really getting bizarre.

"Well, sort of, except not tonight. Tonight it's just the dress rehearsal. You know, when the actors come in, dress up, and rehearse. They pretend to be the dead and talk about their lives as if they were still living."

I continued to stare at him. "That sounds crazy. Besides, the girls would never have picked tonight if they knew the cemetery was going to be so busy."

"Maybe they didn't know," he replied reasonably.

"But wouldn't this sort of thing happen during the day, when people might *normally* come to the cemetery?" Just because he claimed to work here, I still wanted to question his logic.

"No, no," he insisted. "What better time than in the middle of the night, when the cemetery seems to come alive all on its own?"

Just like in the movies. When hands start popping up out of the graves and the zombies chase the high school kids to their gory deaths.

"What time will the *actors . . .* start showing up?" I asked. From the corner of my eye, I swear I saw a shadow flit from a tree toward a collection of gravestones surrounded by a miniature wrought-iron fence. I took a step closer to Paul, truly desperate.

Paul must have seen me flinch a little. "You look a

little nervous, Jessie," he said, beaming me that radiant smile that highlighted his strong white teeth. Was it my imagination or was there some inner light that made him glow? His gaze then swept the expanse of cemetery like the beacon of a lighthouse.

"They've already begun to arrive," he answered, "although they probably don't want to be seen until they're in costume. Why don't we track down your first tombstone while the actors are getting ready? That will give you a chance to get used to the cemetery," he assured me.

"Will people be visiting the cemetery tonight?" I asked hopefully.

Paul shook his head. "No, just the actors tonight. Tomorrow night the people will come. You'll have to come back," he added, as if inspired. "Here, hold on to this."

He pulled a folded piece of paper from his back pocket and handed it to me. I carefully opened it and caught the whiff of the evergreen scent again.

The flyer looked old-fashioned and a bit yellowed. Its fancy font and design looked like the framed ads I saw in the Victorian Shoppe in Manayunk. My mom loved that stuff. A photo of a Civil War general was in the middle of the page. It read:

Saturday,
the 30th day of September,
at 10 p.m.
A TOMBSTONE TEA
at Laurel Hill Cemetery
Tickets for Sale at the Entrance House

"Tickets?" I asked doubtfully.

"Of course. We need to know how many are coming. Hold on to the flyer so you don't forget to come back."

I smiled tentatively as I refolded the paper and put it into my backpack. *Come back tomorrow* had a hopeful ring to it.

"Listen," he whispered, breaking my brief calm. "Can you hear it?"

"Hear what?" I replied, leaning forward, straining to listen.

"The night," he said. "Hear how the night is gently putting the day to sleep? You can if you listen closely—it's like someone slowly snuffing out a candle with a soft breath of air. It's my favorite time of day."

The hair on the back of my neck rose. It was dark and I could see the last of the evening's dying light being chased into the west. The cloaked sky was exhaling one last time to blow the September embers out. A puffed whisper chased past my ear.

"It's so dark all of a sudden," I croaked. I had never noticed the evening fall so quickly. Was it always like this, and I had just never been paying attention?

"It's dark here at night because there aren't any lights. That's why it seems to happen so fast. You can train yourself to see in the dark. Stare at the gravestone ahead of us until you can make out its edges. It helps your eyes to adjust," Paul instructed helpfully, as if he had given this lesson numerous times.

So stare I did, ignoring my trembling knees and demanding that my eyes see the gray whiteness of the stone. Soon I did see it—a ghostly glow—as if the stone had its own inner light. I nodded wordlessly.

"Okay, so what names do you have?' Paul asked, as if aiming to reinvigorate me. "Whose tombstone shall we hunt for first?"

I reached into my backpack, feeling around for the list as I studied his sculpted profile. I noted that closer objects were easier to discern in the cemetery when touched by moonlight. In this shrouded light, his cheeks and chin were softly angular and his nose a strong fine line of bone. His eyes, a melting silver now like fallen sleet, were gentle beneath the firm ridge of his forehead. He could have been the subject of a marble statue, I realized, remembering the bust of the Greek athlete that graced the cover of my Ancient Civilizations book. He was staring now at the collection of stones and statues—some small and some monstrous in size—that seemed to tumble down the hill toward the Schuylkill River.

I shook my head, trying to dispel the cemetery's iconic distractions. I needed to focus if I wanted to get out of here. "Uh, the first tombstone belongs to an Adam Forepaugh, 1830 to 1890. Does that one sound familiar to you?"

He smiled at the name, as if Adam was a good friend. "I know it well," he replied. "We'll need to cut up to the top of the hill and walk along its ridge. Adam has a nice spot overlooking a row of mausoleums and the river. It's the Schuylkill that pleases him most," Paul noted.

"How would you know that?" I asked, my voice rising to a squeak when he impulsively grabbed my hand to guide me along his own irregular path. I felt anxious leaving the safety of my obelisk and began rummaging through my backpack for my flashlight as we trudged along. In the darkness, the trees and tombstones felt especially close, their daytime beauty turned menacing in the night. They morphed into hiding places for small, unmentionable horrors.

"I know many of their personal stories," he replied proudly, not missing a beat. "There are over eleven thousand family plots here, and although I don't know them all, I know most of those that have stamped their mark on our history."

We followed the asphalt driveway, which parted tree-shrouded stones on both sides of us. The crickets were calling again, their insistent chirring vibrating eerily in my ears. Soon Paul had pulled me up some steps, taking us from the path to travel directly among the mounds of the dead.

I was concentrating on watching our feet, which were obscured by the night, the tombstones, and the obelisks that we zigzagged through. The ground felt soft and mushy. The air was fragrant with decomposing leaves and a whiff of the muddy river. The forms of lonely, ink black trees bisected the irregular landscape, mimicking emotions of fear, surprise, or sorrow. Their branches reached out, beseeching the heavens. The white gravestones of the cemetery shined like thousands of moon rocks greedily absorbing the magical light.

I flicked on my flashlight and directed its pathetic beam toward the ground.

"Turn that off!" Paul commanded, swiveling around to grab for the light while I still held it.

I recoiled from him, pulling my free hand from his. My heart wasted no time in acquiring its earlier pace. I could hear my blood swooshing past my ears. I looked back toward the Entrance House, mentally trying to figure out how quickly I would need to run.

"I'm sorry, Jessie," he said, his voice lower and friendly again. "I should have told you it's against the rules. My fault." He extended his hand, seeking forgiveness.

"Against the rules?" I repeated, my voice raw. I had taken another step back. The flashlight, still lit, was behind my back.

"Well, not really." He turned his head for a moment, as if embarrassed. "When the actors are here, they ask that visitors keep their flashlights off and use them only in emergencies. It spoils the atmosphere, as the actors rely on the moon to enhance their...appearance. Their words, not mine," he added hastily, probably in response to the look on my face.

"Really," I said, still gripping my flashlight like a weapon. "So you expect people to tramp around in the dark?" I asked skeptically, trying to calm my fluttering heart.

"Of course not," he answered quickly. "We'll provide candles tomorrow. I don't have one for you, as I didn't expect guests today."

We stood there for what seemed like minutes, our gazes locked, both of us searching for a telling sign from the other.

"Cemeteries weren't always such scary places, Jessie," he ventured, smelling my fear on the air. Again, I noticed a hush in the night sounds, as if the cemetery itself was interested in what Paul had to tell me.

"In the nineteenth century, the cemetery used to sell tickets to people to picnic and spend the day strolling along the beautifully landscaped paths that overlooked the river." His voice had a wistful tone, as if he longed to see those days. "People were glad to escape the heat and the grime of the city. And here they had the chance to spend the day with their lost love ones. It didn't make them feel sad. It made them feel—together again," he ended softly.

"Really?" I whispered, unconvinced, although I turned the flashlight off and returned it to my backpack for safekeeping. The blood in my veins ran cold.

"They did," He nodded. "We're hoping that the actors will draw a big crowd again, to rekindle the old days."

That's when I heard the trumpet like blast. It wasn't an instrument, but the sound of a living creature—a sound heard at the zoo.

Paul smiled in triumph. "Do you hear that, Jessie? We are close to Adam Forepaugh's tombstone. Don't turn away now," he urged. The moon lit his bare arms and face. His eyes were alive with the sound of the creature.

"Is that an elephant?" I asked, again looking wistfully down the hill toward the Entrance House. He extended his hand more insistently, and this time I took it, as I didn't want to be alone here. The cemetery was a world that made its own reality.

"Of course!" He laughed. "It is Adam's elephant. Adam was a circus owner who loved his elephants more than any other creature in the world."

And with that, I allowed him to pull me up the ridge until we reached the top, me breathing heavily from our race. Paul pointed toward a huge black shadow, pacing back and forth at a prescribed distance, as if tethered. The shadow occupied the space between two great mausoleums that were built upon the first earthen terrace on the downhill side of the cemetery. From this vantage point, I could see, hear, and smell the flow of the black Schuylkill River. Its image blended into the overall darkness of the night.

Suddenly, the shadow congealed and lost its fuzzy edges. Now I could see the form of a great creature raise its two pillar-thick legs and the shape of its trunk as it coiled and straightened to let out another blast.

"Come on, Jessie! Let's find Adam!" Paul yelled, pulling me toward the black mass.

How can this be? I wanted to scream. *How can an elephant possibly wander into a cemetery or even be delivered here?*

We ran toward the elephant shadow, snaking down the moonlit hillside across earthen humps that blanketed the skeletons beneath. I allowed Paul to pull me on blind faith, as my eyes were not as adept as his in the dark. We clipped a gravestone or two in this obstacle course because of Paul's zest to reach the actor. When we finally approached a terraced wall, with stone steps that led down to a row of mausoleums, we skidded to a halt and looked down at the patch of grass where the elephant shadow had had its temper tantrum. It had apparently fled. On both sides of us were the two great mausoleums that the elephant had bellowed against. Imprints of the great creature's feet were pressed into the soft earth surrounding us. Far below, the inky Schuylkill stained the landscape.

"Where did he go?" I whispered, half expecting him to come charging from behind one of the mausoleums. I distinctly caught the aroma of hay and dung.

"Why, back to the tent!" a smoky voice shouted. A

figure stepped from the shadows of the larger mausoleum to our left. The name *Forepaugh* stood out in thick marble letters from the face of the stone above its iron door. He held a riding crop in his hand.

"Mr. Forepaugh, sir! Good to see you!" Paul strode up to the silhouetted figure and pumped his hand. I thought it odd that he didn't address the guy by his real name, but maybe these actors were particular about remaining in character. Nevertheless, my heart was still beating a bit too fast and my hands were cold, despite all our running. The actor stepped into the moonlight. He glanced down toward the Schuylkill, as if his elephant had gone looking for water.

The actor, or Mr. Forepaugh, was bald on the top of his head, with a wreath of thick, curly gray hair circling his head from ear to ear and muttonchops of the same color across his cheeks. He wore one of those long coats whose hem ended at his thighs, and he sported a floppy bow tie like Abraham Lincoln's. His pants were a dirty brown color, just like his scuffed boots. He was a plump guy with a twitchy expression and tiny little eyes. I wondered if the tic he had was real or just an affectation.

"Paul, who is the young lady that accompanies you tonight?" His bright eyes looked at me with a hungry curiosity.

Paul didn't seem to notice. He just basked in this guy's company. Maybe they *were* friends.

"This is Jessie, sir. She's on a school assignment to get a number of grave rubbings, and yours is one of them," Paul informed him enthusiastically.

"Is that so!" the actor Forepaugh replied with equal intensity. He lurched toward me as if to get a better look. I gasped involuntarily. The smell of damp earth clung to his clothes. "Well then, first you must hear my story. That's my job, you know."

I nodded as he took me by the elbow and guided me to a stone bench tucked beside the peeling bark of a sycamore tree. Paul slid next to me easily, while the actor literally jumped on the first marble step of the mausoleum in front of us, like a ringmaster primed for the night's performance. The air around us seemed to have grown colder.

"Should I take notes?" I whispered to Paul, depending on him to guide me in our communications with the actor. Silently, I kept repeating to myself that I was completely safe in their company. Paul had told me about the actors and didn't seem nervous at all about me witnessing this drama. All was normal as could be.

"That won't be necessary," Paul assured me. "He's a good storyteller. You'll remember."

And indeed he was. A sudden wind stirred the tree branches above us, and the air carried a teasing scent of horses and canvas and smoking meats. Adam Forepaugh suddenly looked younger.

"Did Paul tell you that I was born a poor boy in Germantown and worked for a butcher when I was only nine years old?" he quizzed me enthusiastically.

"No, he did not, sir," I replied dutifully. "How did you get into the circus business?" I glanced at Paul nervously to make sure that I was supposed to ask questions. Paul looked pleased.

"Horses!" Forepaugh shouted back. "I moved to New York City, got myself into a deal in which I acquired a few hundred horses, and no sooner sold them to the U.S. government for good money, as the Civil War had begun and the government needed horses. But I didn't sell them all." He winked.

I squirmed but took it as my cue to ask another question. "Was it your horses that helped you to start a circus?" I asked.

"Smart girl!" he announced, pointing at me and looking at Paul. By now he was pacing back and forth in front of us, walking his story along. "I sold forty-four horses to Pogey O'Brian for his own circus. When Pogey couldn't pay up, I bought back my horses and his entire circus. I added all sorts of acts and gimmicks—a Wild West show, big-top tents with tigers, bears, and elephants, trapeze artists, and dancers. It turned out that the circus was in my blood." He stopped to catch his breath, or perhaps he was distracted by his own story, as he turned to look wistfully toward the river, in the direction of his elephant. Paul and I remained respectfully quiet, waiting for the actor to remember us.

"We traveled everywhere, all over the United States, packing up our circus wagons as soon as I heard that P.T. Barnum was moving somewhere. I wanted to dazzle the small-town folks, and take their good money, long before Barnum was a puff of dirt on their horizon." He was moving again, punching the air for emphasis, as if P.T. Barnum was directly in front of him.

"You heard the phrase '*There's a sucker born every minute but none of them ever die?*' I attributed that to Barnum. The newspapers were enthralled by our rivalry." He paused again to sigh deeply, as if remembering a time that was truly great—this guy was a good actor.

"I had Barnum beat at his own game," he then whispered to no one in particular.

"But what happened?" I blurted out. By now he had

me mesmerized by the story. "The Barnum and Bailey circus is still famous," I explained. "I saw it two years ago at..."

"Jessie," Paul interrupted, suddenly subdued. "I think it's time you got your first rubbing."

I stared at Paul, surprised at the change in his demeanor. Surely the actor wouldn't take the twenty-first century personally.

"What did you say?" I heard a strained hiss coming from the direction of the mausoleum's stair. I turned to see the trembling Mr. Forepaugh, his fists clenched, his eyes squinted to slits.

"Don't you get it, girlie? I made them what they are. I put the fire in their bellies!" he cried, his own eyes burning with an unnatural intensity. He jumped off the stair to take another step closer to me. "Barnum's circus is built upon the bones of my own creatures. They are what they are because of me!"

He stared at me with mad eyes, daring me to question his assertion. I couldn't help but wonder, *How much are these actors being paid?*

"Jessie, we had better move on, if we plan to find the rest of the tombstones," Paul scolded a bit ominously. Mr. Forepaugh was staring at me, enraged. It was in the discomfort of the moment that I noticed that the cemetery had once again gone silent—no hooting owls, no scissoring sound of bats' wings, or the cry of a small mouse that finds itself in some predator's talons. I didn't even hear the blare of cars in the distance. The cemetery darkness was like a sound-smothering blanket.

I squinted at the foreboding letters jutting from the face of the mausoleum, feeling the panic rumble in my belly. "How can I rub a mausoleum? I can't reach the name," I pointed out breathlessly, not taking my eyes away from the actor.

"You can use the marker behind the mausoleum," Mr. Forepaugh groused. "It should do for your purposes."

"I'll help," Paul said, grabbing my hand and guiding me to a simple stone set close to the earth. If at all possible, this space between the mausoleum and the stone retaining wall was even darker than the night. I ran my hand across the stone to feel for lettering.

"Pull out your paper and lead. I'll hold the paper while you rub," Paul instructed brusquely.

"All I have is crayons," I said, feeling blindly for the small carton in my backpack. "Don't you think that actor is taking this a bit too far? I don't think people like to be yelled at, even when they know it's a show," I whispered.

In the cemetery silence, I could hear the actor muttering to himself, mostly about the "devilish" P. T. Barnum.

"Uh, they're just passionate," Paul replied. I wished I could see his face more clearly. "They want to make the visit to Laurel Hill a memorable one," he continued.

I could hear him flattening my paper as he pulled it taut across the lettering. The sound slapped the air. The aroma of new crayons mixed with the pungent smell of wet grass. I ran my crayon furiously over the entire paper, hoping that I hit enough of the letters to make the rubbing readable.

"That's fine," Paul said, pushing my crayon away and rolling up the paper. "Put this in your backpack and we'll head to the next tombstone." He stood up quickly, pulling me with him. It was obvious that he wanted us out of there.

"Aren't we going to say good-bye to Mr. Forepaugh?" I asked, uncomfortable about the idea of leaving without saying anything, even if he was a crazy actor. I wondered if my mother's manners would be the death of me someday.

"Good-bye, sir!" Paul yelled without looking back, pulling me behind him as we mounted some stairs in the wall to follow a grass path between two neat rows of tombstones.

I turned to see his shadowed figure standing with his hands by his sides, clenching and unclenching his fists.

"Paul, I didn't give you a name yet," I reminded him, doing my best to temper a rising panic. "Will Mr. Forepaugh come after us?" I asked. "He seemed a bit angry," I added.

Paul slowed down, and as he did so, the chatter of the crickets swelled back to life. Or perhaps they only seemed louder as I was paying attention again. Was this, too, my imagination? I need to focus, I scolded myself. I needed to figure out what was going on around here. For once, it wasn't the intrusion of strangers' images that popped into my mind, but the behavior of the real people who were here with me tonight that kept catching me off my guard.

"That's his job, Amy. He's supposed to make you feel as if he is the original Mr. Forepaugh."

"Well, then what did he do with the elephant, Paul? You need to tell me how he really had an elephant here before I totally freak out." I could hear the whining in my voice. Not a good sign.

Paul came to a complete stop to turn to look at me. His eyes shone in the dark, making the tombstones and obelisks that seemed to grow as thick as corn in this section of the cemetery become mere shadows in my peripheral vision. Even the bare tree branches, which had reminded me more and more of gnarled hands ready to grab, faded into the star filled sky.

"Well, I can't tell you *everything,* Jessie," Paul whispered, his voice suddenly gentle and full of sincerity. "But a lot of the actors use special lights and board cutouts to create their illusion. It's effective as long as the visitors are hundreds of yards away. If you get too close, the trick would be ruined."

"Really?" I asked. "But I didn't see any lights or equipment."

"Of course you didn't," He laughed. "Our actors are professional!" He pulled at me again to continue our quest.

"Hmm," I said, suddenly very aware that my hand was still in Paul's very cold one. I wanted to get out of here. I thought of Melanie and the girls, and what they were doing right now. I pictured them in front of the TV at Melanie's house laughing at the idea of me stuck alone in the cemetery. But I wasn't by myself. I was here with a strange guy and an even stranger man. And I knew that Paul was taking me farther into the cemetery. I would never find my way out in the darkness on my own.

"Elisha Kane is next on my list," I said, keeping a whine at bay. And how I wanted to whine. I didn't care about Elisha's tombstone. I wanted to go home.

Paul seemed pleased, though. "You'll like Elisha. He's a good man. One of the best I've known. And his special effects are even better than Mr. Forepaugh's," he promised. "His mausoleum is actually just around the corner."

"You talk about these tombs as if they are a part of a neighborhood," I replied. I shivered at the thought of being surrounded by gravestones every waking day, instead of the yard and house next door.

He looked at me thoughtfully, his chin raised, his head slightly bent as if listening to something. The soft river breeze stroked his hair. He nodded and laughed slightly.

"Jessie," Paul said, stopping again in front of a tall, slender column that looked as if it had broken in two. "This *is* a sort of neighborhood. A neighborhood built from the histories and memories of its residents. That is a very powerful thing," he added sincerely.

I was walking in a surreal world. A world populated by symbols of the dead, be they stone or living actor. Sudden thoughts jolted me. *Is there a witching hour here? Is something or someone wicked stalking Paul and me, luring us into its nightmare world? Is Paul already living there?*

"But this is the present, Paul. We don't belong here. We have nothing to do with these…people." People? Why did I choose that word? They weren't people anymore.

They were bones and dust. Nothing that could hurt us, I reminded myself.

Paul raised a sculpted eyebrow. Something flew—crows—into the tree branches looming above him. I jumped but Paul ignored it. "That's not true, Jessie. History is alive and linked to the present. It's a continuous line. That means we are connected to those who have gone before us."

I shook my head. I didn't think I could take this kind of talk anymore. Not here, surrounded by a city of dead people. I never liked history. Now I knew why. It's all about dead people.

"Paul, I don't need to get any more rubbings. This is just a trick that some stupid girls are playing on me. Can you please take me back?" I asked, striving to sound calm and perfectly reasonable.

"Nonsense," he said. "We're at the second site. Look over your shoulder."

I turned and could do nothing but gasp. For there, on the hillside below us, just beyond the bottom row of mausoleums and the chain link fence that separated the cemetery and the plunging rock encrusted slope to Kelly Drive, was an enormous multisailed ship. Its wooden sides appeared battered, some of its rigging was broken, and torn masts billowed in the wind. It looked crusted over by something, and the next strong breeze coming from the river was so cold that it made me realize that what covered the ship was a skin of ice. The inscription *The Advance* was barely visible on its port bow.

I swallowed hard and began to panic about my sanity. *Might I be having a nervous breakdown?* I almost hoped it were true. That was better than another reality.

"It's Elisha's ship, Jessie. The one that he took and lost on his trip to the Arctic in 1853 in search of the Franklin Expedition." Paul's voice was full of awe.

"That doesn't help me, Paul. I don't know anything about Elisha Kane." Was I crazy to think that a bit more information about his life might make some sense of the ship that I was seeing?

Paul's eyes were bright and he seemed eager to do the telling, almost as if I were a student who was finally catching on.

"Elisha Kane was born in Philadelphia in 1822 and lived an amazing thirty-five years," Paul began, like a true fan. "He went to the University of Pennsylvania to study medicine and became a surgeon, but he also became famous as a geographer, scientist, and explorer."

I kept my focus on the torn masts of the ship that

flapped in the wind, slapping the air like whips. I watched as the ship seemed to tilt toward Elisha's mausoleum.

"But why this ship?" I asked rudely, interrupting Paul's flow. He didn't seem to notice.

"Elisha was invited to join the 1850 search-and-rescue party for Sir John Franklin, the British Arctic explorer, who led two ships on a search for the Northwest Passage—the long-sought shipping channel between the Atlantic and Pacific Oceans. Elisha was the surgeon on *The Advance,* which itself was trapped in the Arctic ice for nine months. But Elisha and the officers and crew of *The Advance* were lucky. They were able to escape and were eventually rescued." Paul became quiet, as if imagining the horror of being trapped by ice. "He went back on a second expedition, but still never found Sir Franklin."

"What happened to him?" I asked, not really wanting to know.

"Subsequent expeditions found evidence—and graves —of the deaths of Sir Franklin and his entire crew. They had apparently abandoned their ice-blocked ship and ultimately died of starvation, cold, and disease. It was quite a mystery and a sensational story in its time. I think Elisha felt he failed Sir Franklin," Paul finished, losing his earlier enthusiasm for the tale.

Such a grim story did nothing for my sense of well being, particularly in a cemetery. I was still focused on the ship on the hillside. "Paul, how could any actor possibly create that sort of special effect here?" I pleaded to know. "Even the air is frigid."

The sound of splintering wood suddenly ripped the air. I screamed. I couldn't help myself.

"Jessie!" Paul cried in alarm. "You can do all sorts of effects with inventions these days. Haven't you been to Disney World? Almost anyone can do this stuff if they have the right equipment."

I strained to listen. Were those the moans of men that I heard wafting from the ship? "But we are in a cemetery, Paul! And these guys are only…local actors, you said!"

"They practice perfection, too!" he exclaimed, sounding surprised that I might think otherwise.

I realized my teeth were chattering from the Arctic cold or the terror running through my veins, I wasn't sure which.

I squatted like a toddler. I covered my face with my hands, wishing this entire place away. I had the odd sensation that hundreds of eyes were staring at my back. I tried to crouch into a smaller ball. That's when I felt the air about my head being buffeted by what sounded like birds' wings. I swung wildly at the air.

"Jessie, stop it! What's wrong with you?" A part of me was relieved to hear that he sounded truly worried.

"Paul, you need to take me back to the entrance, please," I begged him. "I don't want to do this anymore. I was wrong to think I could!"

"But Jessie." Paul dropped down beside me. "This is just a show...to bring people back to the cemetery, not to scare them away," he insisted.

"Well, maybe you need to tell them that they're screwing up!" I yelled, appalled immediately that I screamed such a thing surrounded by. . . .

He shook me lightly by the shoulders. "Open your eyes," he whispered. "The ship is gone."

I slowly opened my eyes. For a few moments my sight had to readjust to the dark but I could readily see that the ship was indeed gone. A decrepit-looking willow tree grew from the terraced hill, its trunk bent like the back of a very old woman. Its long, flowing leaves drifted in the wind, periodically brushing against the top of Elisha's mausoleum like loving fingers.

Suddenly a figure appeared. He seemed to emerge through the wall of the mausoleum, the entrance of which faced the river. "Sir John!" the shadowed figure yelled as he scrambled up the hill, grabbing at some vines and shrubs. He was coming in our direction.

I, too, scrambled to stand, almost knocking Paul to the ground. "It's only Elisha," Paul said. "The actor."

It was too late to run again, so I squinted at the figure, who was doing a cumbersome jog now along the cobble-stoned path between the lowest row of mausoleums and the gently hilled section covered with imposing stones and obelisks.

He was wearing a thickly furred jacket and hood. Bulky mittens were on his hands, and his feet were covered with boots that went above his knees. He cradled an old-looking shotgun under his arm.

"Paul…" I said nervously.

"Don't worry," he replied, standing tall again. "It's just a prop. Dr. Kane!" Paul greeted the man.

He slowed to a stall directly in front of us. He was confused as he looked around at the tombstones and obelisks surrounding him. A thick, dark beard covered his face. His high cheekbones were windburned. His eyes were brightly intelligent as he surveyed Paul and me.

"Paul!" he barked, as if Paul were long lost, too. "Have you caught sight of Sir Franklin and his crew? I'm begin-ning to fear the worst."

I swear I could feel his eyes burning a hole in me. Could he be delirious, I wondered.

"No, I haven't, sir," Paul replied dutifully. "We have only spied your ship."

Dr. Kane was still staring at me. "What about the girl?" he asked keenly. "Might she have been a stowaway?" His question sounded too hopeful to suit me.

"Oh, no, sir," Paul answered quickly. "Jessie is just a visitor, here to collect rubbings."

I wondered how he had figured out a way to bring a zone of cold air with him for the air around us was frigid again.

He took a step closer to me, shifting the shotgun in his hands. He seemed to take a deep breath.

"Shouldn't you be heading out of the Arctic, sir, before the water freezes over and traps your ship?"

He glanced at Paul, as if annoyed. "I plan to die in the harness, my boy, just as my father encouraged." He flashed a brilliant smile, which seemed to momentarily glow in the darkness.

"The girl has a strong life force. I should bring her back to *The Advance*. Could bring us the luck we need," he added, almost wistfully.

"I'm definitely going home now," I announced, stepping back, trying to control the hint of hysteria creeping into my voice. But it was when I felt Paul suddenly stiffen beside me as he grabbed my hand that the hysteria threatened to break my will.

"Dr. Kane, we're going to jog on ahead of you to get a rubbing and be on our way. She's already running a bit late."

And with that, Paul pulled me forward as we literally ran around the guy to sprint to his mausoleum. I turned to take a quick glance and swore I could still see his eyes like tiny points of light in the darkness.

"I don't want the rubbing, Paul! I want to go home, please!" I insisted.

"I'm going to help you with this, Jessie. Some of those actors are a little weird. I apologize for that. But you have nothing to worry about with me."

He held my wrist. His hand was colder than the night. I couldn't run away from him even if I wanted. Unfortunately, my mind wandered to wonder: *How many murders occur in graveyards?* With that, I felt a sudden hatred for Michelle, Melanie, and Jeanne, who were probably having a big laugh at my expense at this very moment. *Does the thought of having me in their group seem so awful that they wanted me dead?* It all seemed crazy.

"Paul!" I snapped, the anger reviving my spirit just a little. "Let go of me. I can walk without your help."

Paul released my wrist as if stung. He slowed our trot to a stop, conveniently in front of the hunchbacked willow tree that was dripping in shadow, its limp branches still fussing over Elisha Kane's mausoleum with each stir of the air. Paul looked me full in the face. He squinted as if he suddenly didn't recognize me.

"What?" I said, trying to keep the annoyance out of my voice. I ignored the licks of fear in my belly as I stared back at him. The moonlight layering his skin lent him a ghostly aura.

"I'm only trying to help," he replied peevishly. "You're the one who came to me. I didn't invite you here." He glanced quickly down the path, in the direction where we had left Elisha Kane standing with his mitten clutching his rifle—a prop, I know that Paul would assure me.

"You have been helpful, Paul." I tried my best to sound gracious again. I knew it was foolish to anger a stranger, particularly a male stranger, in the middle of a cemetery. "But I changed my mind," I added sincerely. "I don't care about joining those girls' stupid club. I don't want to be here in the dark, running from one crazy actor to the next. I just want to go home." I dug my nails into my fists when I felt my eyes tearing up. Last thing I needed to do now was cry.

"But Jessie, it's not about the girls anymore," he said a bit too quietly. "It's about you, about you accomplishing something here. You can do this, and I will watch over you to make sure that no one bothers you anymore."

Were *his* eyes tearing? Paul suddenly seemed like a little boy, despite his sculpted physique. It was the way he stuck his hands in his pockets and stared down at his feet, that reminded me of a lonely child.

"Why do I have to accomplish this tonight?" I whispered, my throat catching on a rebellious emotion. He had hit something in me, something that had been nagging me ever since our move—the terrifying idea that I was a loser.

"To prove to yourself that you can," he answered, his words clipped as if stung by frustration. Now his placid blue eyes seemed to bore into my face.

"I don't know what you mean," I shot back, panicked that my deep, dark fears were so apparent to him. *How could he possibly know of my worries about fitting in at my new school? About kids noticing my reactions to faces and images of people that only I can see?* "Please take me back," I pleaded.

"Jessie, I've worked here a long time," Paul said, fumbling as if he were about to take my hand. I stepped back. "In a cemetery, a living person is like a blinding light, obliterating all the lingering shadows that cling to the world. Your light," he pointed to my eyes, "is flickering with doubt."

The horrible part was, I didn't understand a word he was saying, but I knew he was speaking the truth. By now, my eyes were accustomed to the darkness, but not to the tricks that his stubborn shadows were playing on my mind. A solitary tree, the tombstones, the grass that in the night looked like a dark sea—all implied a terrifying menace. The creatures of the night were silent again. A breeze stirred the otherwise lifeless trees. I could smell the sting of decay in their leaves.

"You wait here," I said. "I can handle the rubbing alone." I was angry and terrified, an emotional combination I never had felt before. If he refused to escort me out of this place, then I was going to finish this chore as fast as I could.

"Elisha's marker is in the front of his mausoleum. Use that for your rubbing," Paul advised with a stern softness.

"Thank you," I said imperiously, clutching my backpack like a weapon. The thought of encountering Mr. Kane's ship again set off my already pounding heart. But I was relieved to see as I crept around the mausoleum wall that the willow tree remained a willow. The marker was easy to find, even in the dark, and I dropped to a squat to start my rubbing. *It is Paul's fault that I am doing this*, I thought bitterly. *Is my heart so weak that even a stranger can ply it?*

Angry tears threatened to blur my vision as I carelessly crayoned over the paper. What did he mean that I had to prove something to myself? As I felt the crayon bumping over the rough surface of the stone, I was flushed with an indignant energy. What normal girl would *not* be afraid to be stuck in a cemetery all night! *And despite my visions, I am a fairly normal girl.* But try as I wanted to, I couldn't miss what Paul had meant. I was lonely. I really wanted to have some friends and be a part of things like I was in Doylestown. So I guess you could say that I was desperate for the life I had only a few months ago. That was why I was willing to do whatever someone asked me to do, as long as they dangled the promise of friendship.

"Are you okay, Jessie?" Paul called, His voice sounded muffled by the night. I glanced around the wall to make sure he stood where I left him as I crammed my rubbing into my backpack. He stood straight, his back to me now, a sentinel as silent and stoic as the sculptures that adorned the hillside. His body tensed.

"How pretty she is," a woman's high, feathery voice called. I couldn't tell from what direction. It seemed to surround us. Paul glanced at me as if to see if I heard it, too. I froze in place, clutching my backpack. If this was another special effect, then these local actors had everything on Disney World.

"Paul, introduce me to your friend, dear." A firm insistence in her voice belied her sweet tone. I plastered myself against the damp mausoleum wall and wondered if covering my ears would help. Her voice was hypnotically soft and plying.

Paul looked at me, and then in the opposite direction, toward the cemetery entrance, mentally calculating whether or not we had enough time to run. I squinted into the distance and saw nothing but the gray darkness.

Apparently Paul decided that there was nothing else we could do. "Come on, Jessie. Jenny wants to meet you." He beckoned me toward him. The doubt on his face almost made me run the other way. Almost. Because there was no way in the world that I would bolt out into the dark cemetery alone.

"Who is it, Paul?" I asked with an edge, as I began to pick my way around a few small tombstones that had long ago become part of the landscape between the walkway and myself. *I don't want to meet anyone else,* I wanted to scream. *I just want to go home.* But I went to Paul, albeit reluctantly.

When I reached him, he was still peering out into the cemetery. The moonlight bathed the thousands of stones in a shower of somber light. The dark shadows cast by the unclouded moon appeared mere slivers at each grave's base. It was within the midst of this ominous light that I saw her. She seemed to spring from the roots of a towering, leafless oak tree.

"Who *is* she, Paul?" I repeated more urgently, as a woman, dressed in what appeared to be a long, white, old-fashioned sleeping gown buttoned all the way to her neck, made her way toward us. She never wavered from her straight course, yet she never slowed to avoid an unfortunately located tombstone or sculpture.

"I told you, it's Jenny," he repeated. But by the edge in his voice, I got the sense that he hadn't expected her or knew what to do with her.

"Yes, but what is her *story*?" I pushed. "What will she say and what should we do about it?" I needed to know what excuse Paul was going to give to the actor to get us out of here. These actors were audience starved, but I wasn't here tonight to feed their hunger for the limelight.

I felt icy cold when Paul replied, "I don't know."

I didn't get to ask him how that could be, because Jenny was approaching us at a good clip, although from all appearances, she was walking. Within seconds, she was standing just a few yards away from us, flanked by one of those broken column sculptures and a tombstone adorned with a flaming torch on top. I knew it had to be my imagination, but the moon loomed larger behind her.

"Hello, Jenny." Paul's tone was cautious. My heart responded in kind. I stood as close to Paul as I could without touching him.

Jenny was indeed wearing a nightgown. Its high collar covered most of her neck, and tiny pearl buttons ran down its front to her waist. She was angularly thin. She looked to be my mom's age—somewhere in her forties—and would have been beautiful if it weren't for the sad, sleepless dark rims that hollowed her eyes. Her blond hair hung straight over her shoulders. It appeared damp in the night air. Bare toes peeked out from beneath her gown.

"She is just my daughter's age," Jenny said, extending her hand as if to touch my face. Her wrist was bony, the veins on the back of her pale hand pronounced. I took a few steps back. Jenny frowned.

"She's not your daughter, Jenny," Paul said with exaggerated cheerfulness. "Her name is Jessie, and she is just visiting the cemetery." There was a rustle of wind in the trees above us. An owl seemed to stop in mid-hoot. For a moment, I thought I heard another voice, a girl's voice like my own, say *Mother* with impatient contempt.

I couldn't pay attention to that. If what I had been feeling was fear throughout this night, what I felt in the presence of Jenny was indescribable. Something alien seemed to clamp over my heart. I could taste the darkness on my tongue.

I must run, I told myself. With or without Paul, *I must run.* But my feet didn't know how to comply. This actor, this woman playing Jenny, didn't need any special effects. She had an eerie, translucent glow about her that said she was not of this world. And she was barefoot, on this cool September night, leaving a meager impression of herself on the damp grass.

"I disagree, Paul." Jenny sounded annoyed. She looked over her shoulder slowly, as if she were expecting some more company. "Why don't you let me talk to her? Surely you have other things to do."

"I can't, Jenny," Paul stammered. "She is our guest, and she must leave here tonight when she has done what she came to do."

I realized that Paul was trembling. His mouth looked hard, and he was staring at Jenny as one would stare at a wild animal. I held my breath. The blood pounding against my ears rasped shrilly like hundreds of unseen voices, but only Jenny stood before us.

She turned her large, deep set eyes upon me and smiled. It was then that something grabbed me. Not on the outside, but on the inside. My lungs were gently squeezed; my blood skipped though my veins. I swore I felt something tug at my very life.

"Stop it, Jenny," I heard Paul plead, but he suddenly sounded far away.

I couldn't catch my breath, and everything—the cemetery, Jenny, and Paul—seemed to fade around me. All was suddenly a startling, cold fog. I could taste the sea against my lips and felt the sting of harsh salt air against my face. I could hear bells and screaming in the distance. Something inside me was crumbling.

"You can't have her, Jenny!" someone shouted, and the fog suddenly disappeared. Paul was dragging me up the pathway.

"We're going to the top of the hill, and then we'll double back to the Entrance House," Paul yelled.

I couldn't really focus. I felt caught between two

worlds—Jenny's fog-enshrouded one and the surreal world of the cemetery.

I didn't answer Paul. Instead I tried to concentrate on the concrete pathway, which softly reflected the moonlight as its carpet. On both sides of us we passed a dizzying array of tombstones. The kaleidoscoping graves were making me dizzy.

I wanted to ask Paul to slow down before I stumbled, but when I looked up it was not Paul's hand that I held but Jenny's cold, bony one. The cemetery was gone again, replaced by the chilling, heavy sea fog.

In my terror I could say nothing as Jenny turned her long white face to me, her unnatural smile mimicking a maternal satisfaction that I have seen on my own mother's face. "We're almost there, dear. The lifeboats are waiting. Don't let go like you did before," she warned.

I realized that the concrete pathway was gone and that we were running across the wooden deck of a ship. People, invisible in the fog, were screaming, shouting, wailing, or begging God's mercy. An explosion somewhere beneath us caused the deck to lurch. There were more screams, more desperate than the last, as the sound of fog-concealed bodies splashed into the water.

My panic was raw. My fingers and toes were numb

with the cold. I tried to pull away from Jenny. To stop. I wanted to get back to Paul and the cemetery. But Jenny wouldn't have it.

"Are you tired, dear? We must not delay. They're holding the last lifeboat for us," she assured me. Her bearing was resolute yet she threw me a look over her shoulder that was almost giddy. She was going to save her daughter, despite me and the past.

It was then that I saw a girl my age with long dark braids falling over each shoulder. She wore ribbons in her hair and a nightgown like her mother's. She stood alone on the bare, wet deck, and the loose riggings of a sail convulsed in the wind behind her. But neither her hair nor clothes took notice of the wind as she stood with her arms crossed, her face without emotion, as if bored with the scene. I wanted to call out to her.

But something grabbed my free hand.

Jenny roared as if hell were interfering. The fog began to swirl around us, raising her wet hair in frozen tendrils about her head.

"Leave her!" she screamed as I was being pulled back into the cemetery. With another hard yank, I had one foot on the deck and the other on cottony soil. But within moments, I was flat on my back, the cool dewy grass of the cemetery dampening my jeans and sweatshirt. Paul was straddled over my waist, as if we had been wrestling.

"What are you doing?" I screamed at him, fearing that surely I was going out of my mind.

Paul's face was a scramble of panic and confusion. He was as pale and luminous as Jenny.

"I'm trying to save you!" he yelled back, jerking his head around in all directions, as if whatever he was saving me from could come from any of them. He pulled me up and I clung to him.

"Don't let her get me again," I begged. "I don't want to die with her on that ship."

I knew I sounded insane, but Paul simply nodded his head and then raised it, as if smelling the air like an animal. Again, the cemetery was oddly silent. From the top of the hill, the tombstones glowed like thousands of pearls against the dark velvet grass. In a photograph, these stone-hewn jewels would be stunning against this otherworldly backdrop. But not now.

The black-stained trees pantomimed their own fear and horror as they seemed to rage against the moon-brushed sky. In the distance, at the bottom of the gray chalk driveway that serpentined down the hillside, among graves, obelisks, and mausoleums, lay the Entrance House like an innocent chaperone, oblivious of the antics of its long-dead occupants.

"We're running straight to the bottom," Paul said. "Where's your backpack?"

I looked around my feet. I didn't see it on the ground or on the concrete walkway but I no longer cared about it. I just wanted to get out of here.

"I don't know. It doesn't matter," I assured him. "Will you please just take me out?"

"Come on." Paul grabbed my hand and, as he did, Mr. Forepaugh and Dr. Kane suddenly sprang from the earth twenty yards down the hill. They stood like vigilante guards on opposites sides of the driveway, both annoyed and shaking their heads.

"What do you think you're doing, Paul?" Mr. Forepaugh whined. "She hasn't finished telling me some more secrets about that pompous ass Barnum." Forepaugh yanked at the hem of his topcoat and nervously played with the cuffs of his sleeves.

"Indeed!" Elisha Kane added. "I'm sure the girl is a stowaway. I insist that you give me the opportunity to interrogate her about the missing Franklin!" His frozen beard quivered with outrage. He swayed in the blasts of a ferocious wind that only he could feel.

"Paul!" I hissed. "These people aren't actors, are they?" I didn't really want to hear him say no.

"We can outrun them. Come on!" And again he began running like a creature that could see in the dark. We dashed between tombstones and obelisks, completely avoiding the driveway where Forepaugh and Kane were stamping their feet in a tantrum. I paid no mind to the tree branches that slapped my face and arms, nor to the soft ruts in the ground that threatened to swallow an ankle. I tried to ignore the expressions on the faces of the angels that we came eyeball to eyeball with before Paul would cut a new path away from the almost inevitable collision.

We were halfway down the hill when I began to feel my right leg go numb as it suddenly was encased by the sea. Jenny and her fog had caught me again.

The shocking cold of the ocean constricted my lungs. I forgot how to breathe. I was doggy-paddling, just trying to keep my head above the water as the fog lay on the ocean surface like a cloud. I couldn't see anything. All I could hear were the screams and dying moans of people in the water. Their disembodied cries ramped up my own terror.

Something bumped against my shoulder. I swirled around to see Jenny in an otherwise empty lifeboat. She thrust her hand out. Her wet hair clung to her sunken cheeks.

"Give me your hand, Amy dear, before it's too late. The ship is about to slip beneath the waters and it will drag you with it."

She tilted her head and smiled as if I were a dim-witted child. Even if I wanted to reach out to her, my arms were too numb to lift out of the water. I was thinking about allowing the ship to take me with it.

Jenny must have read my thoughts, because she frowned, twisting her face into a scary crossness. She stood up in the boat, stood up without causing it to rock in the slightest. Her nightgown was flapping in the wind, pressing against her scrawny body. It was then that I saw the wave roaring toward us, eclipsing the horizon so that all that was visible behind it were the stars. I wanted to scream, to warn her, but I couldn't. Instead, I slowly sank beneath the surface.

"Jessie!" I heard Paul yell. Someone then slapped me on the face. "Come back to me!"

I took a deep breath, thankful to be breathing cemetery air instead of ocean water. Paul was standing in front of me, his hands on my shoulders, his gray, steely blue eyes anxiously searching my face.

❧

"My God! She almost had you!" he yelled, as if he were angry with me. I was still so cold, yet when I felt my jeans and sweatshirt, they were dry.

"I want to go home, Paul." I absently looked at the ground around me, ensuring that I really was surrounded by solid earth. I was moving and thinking in slow motion, as if the sea had numbed my brain.

"You're trembling," he said, his voice now mellowed with concern. He quickly unbuttoned his flannel shirt and wrapped it around my shoulders. His smooth, bare chest and shoulders glowed warmly in the moonlight.

"You'll be cold," I said, clutching his shirt like a magic charm.

He shook his head. "I don't get cold. And don't worry. I'll find your bag later. Come on."

He swooped me up in his powerful arms and began jogging down the driveway. I felt like a tiny child watching the procession of phantom tombstones glide by us. Still there was no sound, not even the whisper of a breeze as it trifled with the branches of the nearly bald trees. I kept my sights on the columned Entrance House and on the archway that slipped beneath it—the door to the outside world. I focused on the house, glad to see it magnify slowly in size.

"Oh, no," Paul said into my ear and stopped. Suddenly, they were all in front of us, a barrier of bodies—Jenny, Forepaugh, Kane, and many others—men, women, and children in various clothes and sizes—all looking at us expectantly as they blocked the driveway exit.

"Paul," I whined as he lowered me to the ground. "What do they want?"

"They want...to be noticed, I think. They have not done this since..." he whispered, and then trailed off.

I couldn't help but look into their faces. All shared the pinched, pale, hollowed-eye look of Jenny. But that's where the similarity ended. There was an old man, hunched over, dressed in black tails as if he was coming from a wedding. Wisps of gray hair floated about both ears. He bowed and gave me an odd smile when our eyes met.

Beside him were two girls, about my age, dressed as if they had stepped from a page of the novel *Little Women*. They held hands, leaned in toward each other, and giggled until I looked away.

Near Mr. Forepaugh, a woman holding a baby swayed back and forth as if to rock the child to sleep. Both she and the baby were dressed in long nightgowns. Her brown hair tickled the baby's cheek as she leaned in to it and cooed.

Two boys in knickers and caps stared at me with the same bright eyes as Paul. There were men dressed in suits and women in black dresses and hats, huddled together on the other side of Mr. Kane as if they were at a cocktail party. But they, too, stared at me with an uncomfortable intensity, as if waiting for me to make a move. I froze.

"Jessie." Jenny broke the silence. "Stay with us." Then the others started, chanting my name. "Jessie, Jessie."

I covered my ears but couldn't stop looking at their faces. The street lights behind them flickered like fireflies.

"Paul, these people are dead, aren't they?" I asked, surprised by my resigned calmness. It almost seemed easier accepting this truth than trembling from the fear of it. Not one of them moved toward us, although they seemed to collectively lean in our direction.

Paul looked from them to me. "They're not ghosts, Jessie." His eyes beseeched me to believe him, "At least not in the sense that you are thinking of..."

Mr. Forepaugh stepped forward. He ran one hand across his bald pate and fiddled with his floppy bow tie as if he were going to make a speech. The others moved closer to him, pressing against one another.

"My dear," Forepaugh began insinuatingly. "We don't mean to scare you." He bobbed his head reassuringly.

"You warm us, like a crackling fire. We're cold here, cut off . . ."

"What he means . . ." Paul interrupted, but was cut off by Elisha Kane, who stepped in front of Adam Forepaugh.

"It's your spirit, child." Dr. Kane glanced around at the others, expecting them to nod agreeably. "Your life is like a brilliant star in this darkness." He rubbed his mittened hands together, as if trying to warm them.

"Where are the others?" I heard myself ask, appalled that I spoke out loud. Paul stiffened beside me and seemed to hold his breath. "There are hundreds of graves here." I glanced over my shoulder, almost expecting a body to be standing over each humped mound of earth.

It was Jenny who was instantly in front of me. She tilted her head and smiled. Her lips were thin and blue, her skin translucent where it spread over her high cheek-bones. Before I could pull back, she grabbed my hands and placed them against her heart. Her hands felt as cold as stone.

"We're not that sort of ghost, Jessie," she whispered. "It's the darkness of the past, a darkness that obliterates the gleam of the after light that keeps us here." Jenny licked her lips expectantly, as if light were nourishment. "Stay with us, Jessie."

They began to crowd around me and my heart seemed to slow in the crush of cold air. It was suddenly hard to breathe, as if my life were being squeezed out of me.

"Paul!" I cried, my panic in full force again as the bodies around me seemed to dissolve into shadowy vapors that clung loosely to their human forms. Paul was outside of this fog. I could see him pressing against it, struggling to thrust his arm toward me.

Somehow he reached my hand. I felt him grab it and pull me forward. The air clung to my body like vines as I broke free. Paul was running with me, our feet pounding against the cobblestoned driveway as we ran beneath the arch to the black iron gate that I had slipped through only hours before.

"Get out!" he yelled, pushing me toward that gap between the iron posts of the gate and the fence. "Hurry!"

I hesitated, looking into Paul's blue eyes and then to the world behind him—thousands of tombstones throbbing in the ethereal light on hillsides that seemed to lap against the Schuylkill River beneath the moon-filled sky. How many of those who were fighting against some darkness would Paul have to deal with?

"What about you?" I asked breathlessly. "Shouldn't you come, too?"

He smiled. Just barely. "I can handle it. It's my job. But I want you to promise me something."

"What?" I nearly screamed, as I was incapable of speaking in a normal tone under the circumstances.

"That you'll come back when you're ready." Incredibly, he leaned forward and gave me a quick kiss on the cheek. "Now go!" he ordered and then gently pushed me through the small space in the gate that was my passage to the outside world.

All was silent. Paul and the others had vanished before I even turned around. The Entrance House stood before me, completely alone, eerily quiet. The row houses behind me were dark with sleep. No car traveled at the moment on Ridge Avenue. Only the streetlight directly above my head buzzed with an overcharged intensity. I clutched Paul's flannel shirt like a talisman as I stood in shock. Ghosts— and a kiss. Instead of crying, I began to run home.

———— ·◎· ————

The cemetery looked safe in the warm sunshine, as did the streets and houses that fronted its entrance. A part of me calmed down just a little as my mom swung the car through the now open and inviting iron gates, onto the chalk white cobblestoned driveway, and beneath the wooden arch of the Entrance House that I had raced through just the night before.

When I reached home last night, after running through the deserted, dark streets of East Falls, I told my parents everything. Well, not *really* everything. I didn't tell them about Paul and the . . . spirits. But I did tell them about the dare, and how I really wanted to get all those rubbings so that I could be a part of *the* group. They weren't as mad as I thought they would be, even though it was well after midnight, and I had woken them both up by banging on our front door. I couldn't help myself. I kept expecting to see Jenny floating behind me all the way home.

My mom just held me, and the familiar smell of her, in sweats that doubled as pajamas, was soothing.

"I wish you had told us, Jessie. We forget how difficult it is to be in a new school, especially at your age." She brushed my damp bangs away from my eyes. "You need to tell us when something is bothering you."

Dad was hovering over her shoulder. His hair was mussed from running his hand through it. He had a mug of coffee in his hand.

"Jessie, what were you thinking?" he sputtered. "Running around in the middle of the night . . ."

"Mark, please," my mother interrupted. "Not now. Why don't you make us some hot chocolate? We can talk about this tomorrow."

He went silent, but didn't look happy. He drained his mug before disappearing into the kitchen.

It was the next morning, when the sun shot its beams through my window and across my bed, that I was ready to say that I wasn't *that* lonely, certainly not lonely enough to need friends who were such jerks. I just needed to be patient. I would find true friends who would not make fun of me or send me alone to a cemetery at night.

It was just after noon when the call came from Laurel Hill. One of the groundskeepers had found my backpack. My student ID was in it.

I didn't want to go with my mother to pick it up, but she insisted.

"Come on, Jessie. This will be good for you to see the cemetery in the sunlight." Her purse was already slung over her shoulder and the car keys were in her hand. "You know how our imaginations can run wild, especially in a cemetery," she said cheerily. "Let's check it out together."

I wasn't so sure. "Okay, but I reserve the right to stay in the car if the place still creeps me out." But maybe she was right. Maybe I did need to see it in the daylight to put everything into perspective. I thought about Paul's plea to me to come back when was ready. I felt myself redden, embarrassed by the notion that I was keen on a ghost.

It did look different, I realized, despite my spastic heart, which continued to quiver as we parked on the cobblestoned driveway. The cemetery rolled out in front of us, a series of gentle hills blending into the horizon. In the sunlight, the tombstones and obelisks looked like simple stones and statues surrounded by a carpet of green, dew laden grass. Even the leafless trees looked harmless in their nakedness beneath the lively blue sky. Clusters of people, or single strollers, walked among the various pathways and graves, as if the cemetery were nothing more than a lovely park. I shivered, despite myself, when I looked over to the curly-haired cast iron angel—Amy Halprin's angel—who I had clung to last night, until Paul had spied me. Paul... *will I see him here today*? My stomach seemed to flip.

I could feel my mother's intense stare even through her sunglasses. I always found this annoying as I stared back, only to be confronted by my own reflection. We both had short dark hair and freckles splashed across our nose and cheeks. My nose—like her nose—turned up a little, not enough to be perky, she assured me. She, like

I, was athletic—tennis is her sport—and we share thin, supple builds that allow us to stretch for a wayward ball. But my dad says that our eyebrows are the most expressive parts of our faces. He swears they are synchronized, simultaneously shooting up whenever we question the accuracy of one of his long stories. My mother, unlike Jenny, looked exactly like me.

She paused before she opened her car door. "Are you okay, Jessie? You look a little spooked."

Appropriate choice of words, I thought. Instead I quickly opened my door and mumbled, "Yeah, I'm okay. Let's just get my backpack."

She placed her hand on my shoulder as we rang the doorbell of the Entrance House office. Funny, I hadn't noticed the office on the left side of the building last night. Its glass windows overlooked the driveway beneath the arch. Potted plants in vases that looked like giant urns flanked the door.

A tiny old woman in a colorful plaid skirt, pink polo shirt, and red glasses covering half her face opened the door. Her short white hair stood up from her scalp like fluffy smoke. Her smile was very kind.

"Oh, are you Jessie Maher?" she asked, as if thrilled to solve some mystery. Her voice rang high like a dinner bell. "My name is Mary. *Miss* Mary, the young people call me."

"Hello" I nodded, completely embarrassed. *I'm the idiot who wanted to spend the night here.*

"And I'm Jessie's mother, Joan," my mom said, helping her open the screen door, which whined with the effort. "Thank you so much for calling us."

Miss Mary waved us in as she shuffled toward an opening in the office counter.

"It was my pleasure," she beamed. "I am always so happy to know that young people still enjoy the cemetery. Do come again," she invited as if we truly were attending a tea party.

Miss Mary disappeared for a moment behind the counter as she bent to look for something. Then she popped back up again.

"I must have left it in the back office. I'll be just a minute," she promised.

Mom was already sauntering about the office, peering at the old black-and-white framed photos that covered most of the walls.

"Look at these, Jessie," she encouraged, reaching to grab my elbow. "All of these famous Philadelphians are buried here—Rittenhouse, Widener, Elkins, Strawbridge, and Sully. And so many Civil War generals, including George Meade, the Union general at Gettysburg. This is like looking through the pages of a history book!"

Unlike me, my mother *loved* history. But I found myself peering closely at the grainy photos, looking to see if I recognized anyone from last night.

That's when I saw Paul. Or someone who looked exactly like Paul. He was standing beside an open grave, leaning on a shovel, dressed in bulky jeans, boots, and a flannel shirt much like the one I still had in my possession. His hair looked dark with sweat, but his smile was easy and friendly. I could make out his muscled frame beneath his shirt. The photo was dated in the bottom righthand corner—1906.

"Jessie, are you sure you're all right? What are you gasping at?" My mother leaned closer to the photo of Paul. "He was very good looking," she said, touching the frame to right it.

"Very handsome," Miss Mary agreed, causing us both to jump. She had crept right behind us without making a sound.

"What's his name?" I asked in a whisper.

She cocked her head. "Such a sad story," she tisked. "Paul, Paul O'Malley. Died from typhoid fever when he was just sixteen."

"But that's impossible," I said softly, unable to stop staring at the photo. Although it was a faded black and white, Paul's eyes still held their own brilliance, like the cartoon glimmer of a star.

I could feel my mother peering at me. The old lady managed to step between us.

"A strange story, too," she added, a tone of secrecy wrapping around her words. "His parents were spiritualists—people who believe that when a person dies, their soul moves on to the spirit world and resides there until they are able to reach God." Her blue eyes were bright behind her glasses—her own spirit twinkling at me.

"While the dead are in this spirit world, they can communicate with the living. At least that's what they believed," she added hurriedly, noticing my mother's open mouth of protest.

My heart was beating fast. My hands felt clammy. "Did Paul's parents talk to him after he died?" I asked, ignoring my mother's pursed lips.

She shook her head. "They seemed to disappear from the area when he died. We believe that Paul is buried here somewhere, but oddly we don't have any record of it. His parents must have been heartbroken."

She paused and delicately pushed at her fluff of white hair.

"Ah, I see you have Jessie's backpack," my mother interrupted, her voice forced full of that fake cheeriness she liked to use when she was uncomfortable. I knew she was bothered by this talk of spirits, as she had spent half the night and this morning convincing me that all I need to fear is my own imagination.

"Yes, indeed," Miss Mary twittered, plopping the backpack on the counter. "I hope you don't mind," she said, raising her eyebrows, "but we did need to go through it to determine its owner."

"Of course," my mother interjected. "We very much appreciate your calling us."

Miss Mary looked at me curiously. My heart skipped a beat. Was it the rubbings that made her look at me as if I had something to hide?

"I only mention this because I happened to notice an old Tombstone Tea flyer, an event that the cemetery used to host until the 1920s. I was wondering where you had found it."

Her question hung in the air.

"I can't remember," I said vaguely. "But you can have it . . . for the cemetery," I added quickly.

Her smile burrowed into her cheeks. "Thank you, my dear. This will be a wonderful addition to our historical collection." She zipped up my backpack and handed it to me, carefully placing the flyer under a cherub paperweight.

"Did you know that we have been trying to reestablish the Tombstone Tea tradition?" Miss Mary asked, her stare focused on the flyer. "People would spend the entire day visiting their dead in the cemetery, bringing along picnic baskets. The cemetery would serve tea, right here in this very office." Her voice had assumed a more serious timbre.

This all sounded way too familiar, remembering Paul's own fondness for the cemetery.

My mother was looking at us both as it we were coconspirators. Her mouth was open again as she searched for the right question.

"Would you mind signing our guest book?" Miss Mary asked, her voice on pitch again, as if sensing the need for a diversion. "And perhaps, Jessie, if you and your classmates are looking for a special credit project, you might think about working on a Tombstone Tea with us." She tilted her head and gave me the brightest, most encouraging smile.

I nodded and I think I whispered, "I'll think about it."

My mother was still searching her bag for a pen to sign

the guest book. She peered at the two of us curiously, as if trying to figure out my real connection to this place.

"I'll wait outside," I said, grabbing my backpack before I quickly pushed open the screen door into the soft sunlight.

I allowed my gaze to slowly wander over the panorama before me. The tombstone-laden hills seemed to roll weightlessly into the horizon, the whites of their stones clear and sharp in contrast to the golden grass and rich brown of the trees. Birds chirped brightly, as if thrilled with the warm autumn day. Nothing about the cemetery appeared somber or scary. It seemed a completely different place. *Could I have possibly imagined it all?* But the Tombstone Tea flyer told me otherwise.

I could hear my mother's voice, polite and serious, talking to Miss Mary, whose own voice was high and musical by any comparison. What was my mother probing about? That's what she did, my dad liked to say, dissect a situation for all it's worth.

Maybe she was asking where my backpack was found, about the old flyer that was in it. She'd want to know how her daughter had come across such a thing.

I sat on the curb of the Entrance House sidewalk, my back to the screen door and my mother inside. I could smell the yellow chrysanthemums that burst from the clay flowerpots that bordered the sidewalk in a deliberate attempt to make this place like a home.

But it was anything but like home. It was a place occupied by spirits who are not ready to move on. And then there was Paul, still caring for these people as he did when he was alive. I thought of the photograph of Paul on the wall—Paul in 1906 looking exactly as he did last night. I wished I could have it.

I fingered the straps of my backpack thoughtfully as if the answer lay within its contents. I unzipped it and felt for what I knew to be there—the pack of crayons, my flashlight, and the paper I brought for my rubbings. But unlike last night, the paper was neatly rolled together.

I pulled it out and looked at the smooth white roll in the bright daylight. My mother's voice still hummed behind me.

I swallowed once before I unwound the paper, pulling its edges taut so I could read them. I pulled each paper layer away one by one.

There were the two rubbings I obtained—Adam Forepaugh and Elisha Kane. A shiver went through me just thinking about them. But there were more rubbings, names that were on the list that the girls had given me but carved on graves that I did not reach—Price, Meade, Wister, Lewis, Pemberton, Owen, Knowles, Painter.

I sucked in my breath as my fingers traced the name and epitaph on the last rubbing.

Paul O'Malley

Speaker for the Dead

A Listener for the Living

A light breeze stirred my hair and caused the chrysanthemums to tremble. My ear seemed to be tickled by a whisper. "We can do better tonight."

With my heart beating hard, I stood up and took a deep breath. Maybe that Tombstone Tea thing might be worth checking out. I turned and opened the door to ask Miss Mary for a little more information, before I changed my mind.

DO NOT USE—TYPHOID!

The Betrayal

Dawn had just cracked the horizon, but already the early June humidity pressed against the pores of my skin. This was my favorite spot, this little mound of cemetery that rolled away from Elisha's mausoleum like an earthen wave. From here, beneath a mammoth willow tree that seemed to gain great amusement at tickling your bare skin with its branches, I could look over the entire Schuylkill River Valley.

Elisha's spot perched on a cliff at least two hundred feet above the river drive. Even now, at this early hour, I could see the horse-drawn coaches and open wagons trotting to and from the city. The hooves of the horses and the wheels of the carriages each churned up their own little tempests of dirt.

The carriages belonged to men of commerce, I surmised, as their drivers were dressed in formal black morning coats and homburgs pushed down upon their heads, covering the tips of their ears. The wagons, filled with a variety of materials—water and sewer pipes, hay for stables, baskets of fruit and other groceries—were driven by men in overalls and engineers' caps, the uniform preferred by the tradesmen. If I had to choose a lot in this life, I would jump in the seat of the wagon. These men lifted their hats in greeting and called out one another's names. Their jobs did not seem to confine their spirits.

Beyond the road was the muddy Schuykill, fast and full of tree limbs that it collected from last night's heavy rain. The scullers that usually plied the river like water striders were absent today due to the furious flow. An aroma of cool, wet mud tinged the air. Across the river, Fairmount Park rose and reclined, its wildflower covered hills bursting with fiery reds and yellows amid the staid evergreens. The dome of Memorial Hall hovered in the distance like a cap.

I liked to arrive early to work, when the only noise that reached my ears was the card-shuffling sound of insect wings and the joyful tweeting of the birds, which seemed to share my love for the dawn. At this hour, the cemetery was free of the mourners and the strollers, who would surround me sometimes while I dug a grave or pruned a tree. Mr. Hogan, the cemetery manager, tried to shield me by sending me to the far reaches of the cemetery during the height of the day, when lines to gain entrance to the cemetery piddled down Ridge Avenue. He knew their neediness drained me.

"Unlike ours, Paul?" Elisha whispered in my ear. I could sense the smile buried beneath his frosted beard.

I sighed. When I answered them, I spoke out loud. It made me feel a bit more normal. "You do not cling, Elisha. Or gnash against your death like many of the others. You have left no scars on me." I inspected my slightly tanned forearms, scarred and carved with pin-like scratches from others who were less resigned.

"Ah, that's because I died in the harness. I have no real regrets now, though I fear if I remain in this world I just may acquire some."

The thought of Elisha the explorer suddenly feeling qualms over the choice of his career unnerved me. "Well, just make sure you do move on, then. You would be a bit much to handle." I was only half joking. Elisha's energy was fierce.

I grabbed the shovel that I had left leaning against Elisha's mausoleum. The first grave that I had to dig this morning was for a young woman. I did not want to be near the site when the funeral took place tomorrow. The spirits of the young were so unpredictable.

I nodded my good-bye at the mausoleum and took the few stairs carved into the high hillside terrace that led to the cobblestoned driveway that wound toward the Entrance House. This girl was from a good family. Her grave could be seen through Mr. Hogan's office window, a guarantee that it would be well taken care of.

As I looked over the thousands of tombstones that appeared to be scattered across the earth's green cover like winter's first snowflakes, I remembered to hum a church hymn that would dampen any roving spirit. Although my mother could not see the dead, she knew of all the tricks to deal with them when necessary. I had work to do and could not listen to their unrealistic appeals.

It was my mother who opened up my senses, who taught me the spiritualism that she and my father embraced two years ago, after my grandmother died. My mother had been her only child and she soon began sensing my grandmother's presence in the house or at her side, particularly at times of the day when they had often been together—knitting in the morning, going to the market at noon, baking bread in the early evening.

But my grandmother never *appeared* to my mother unbidden. It was only after my mother joined a group of spiritualists—other neighborhood women who had lost someone dear to them—did she actively learn to conduct a séance to summon a person in the spirit realm. Spiritualists believe that the souls of men and women continue to walk this world in a place that's neither earth nor heaven. Those souls often linger close to earth, searching to resolve a tragic loss, act of betrayal, or any event that shattered their hearts. Such powerful emotions reside long after their owner's physical being.

Normally, these spirits do not communicate with the living until called, and only respond when they are willing. But I don't need to search for them. They come to me unbidden. Elisha compares me to a divining rod for spirits. I still don't know whether it's a curse or a blessing, although for those who lost someone, it seems to bring a kind of hysterical joy. But for the dead, I'm still not sure. Reaching out to them seems to tether their spirits indefinitely.

Something changes in a person when the wall between the living and the dead is breached. My fear of death lessened, yet my appreciation for the solidness of real life—the firmness of a handshake, the coolness of the wind, the cloying smell of wilting grave flowers—brought my heart to a more urgent beat. I still don't know if this is good or bad.

My first encounter was with my grandfather. It was a

September day, the light of which was already dying with a pink intensity. The air smelled of brittle, castaway leaves when I slipped into our brownstone. My mother and father were seated at the small table in the parlor, holding hands across its width, the light of a candle casting shadows across their faces. My mother's hair was swept up in a chignon with long brown tendrils curling around her checks. Her pale blue eyes were focused on the flame. My father, the gray in his beard less noticeable in the twilight, was staring intently at her, as if willing her to speak.

"I'm home," I whispered, which seemed to break the spell, for they both looked up at me with pleasure on their faces.

"Sit down, Paul," my mother invited, briefly letting go of my father's large hand to pat the pillow on the chair beside her. "We think you're ready."

"Are you sure?" I asked, the beat of my heart rising. Although I knew what my parents practiced, they had been careful to shield me from it. My father had insisted that I had to be of an age to reach my own conclusions. At sixteen, he believed that I was a man.

I was their only child, a loner by nature, not because I wasn't sociable with other people. I just had a *serious* nature, my father liked to say. He envisioned me becoming a great teacher and was saving some of his earnings from his accounting job with the Baldwin Locomotive Works to pay for my schooling at the University of Pennsylvania once I graduated high school. I wasn't sure about this. I liked working at the cemetery.

"We don't want to pressure you, son. We just want to see how—receptive—you are." My mother grabbed my hand as I sat down beside her. Candlelight was kind to her, and I caught my breath as I saw a reflection of myself in her face. "At any moment you feel—awkward—do not hesitate to tell us."

I nodded. My parents were aware that spiritualists like themselves were often viewed as eccentric by more tolerant people. Our pastor, once he became aware of their newfound practice, had quietly asked them to leave our church. Most Christians could not abide this sharing of the earth with those who were supposed to be dearly departed.

"Take our hands, son, and focus your gaze on the light of the candle. Open up your mind to a world we have yet to cross into," my father instructed. His lips were pursed and his thick dark brows lay heavy over his eyes, an expression he acquired whenever he deliberately concentrated.

I closed my lids when they tilted their chins to the ceiling. Once or twice I stole a glance around the room to see if anything had changed, but only the shadows cast by the flickering candle showed any life in the room. Finally, I allowed my mind to drift almost to the edge of sleep. It was then that I felt his presence.

He had often smelled of the outdoors, for unlike his son, he was a laborer. His clothes held the scent of chilled air and pipe smoke. It suddenly filled the room. An image of his large-knuckled hands that so easily swung a sledge-hammer or led a horse spooked by a cat into the stable without fuss filled my head. As a young child, I was mes-merized by the power of his hands. It made sense that they would be the first things to make themselves known to me.

"Paul, are you watching over your parents, boy?" he asked, his voice still carrying the lilt from his homeland. "I can't seem to get to them."

"I am, Grandfather," I answered eagerly, just as I greeted him as a child when he burst through our doors, always unannounced. I had spoken out loud and felt both my parents jump in their seats. My mother gave a little cry. Otherwise, they didn't say a word but they held my hands with a numbing grip.

He said no more, and I didn't know what to ask. This was my first communication, which seemed to break down all walls between me and the spirit world. But at that moment, we both seemed to take comfort in the knowledge of each other's presence. When the scent of smoke and wind disappeared, I knew he was gone. After this, I never needed to formally summon an all-too-willing spirit who demanded attention.

⁂

I was not anxious to reach the girl's grave site, but I was relieved that the funeral was a day away. She would be at home still, resting in her coffin amid sitting room furniture now shoved ungraciously against the walls. I couldn't help but wonder when the spirit decided to walk. Was she still sleeping in a sense? Or did the prospect of so many familiar faces, almost unrecognizable now in their distress, propel her spirit to vault from her body?

The grave site was just around a bend of the cobbled driveway of the Entrance House. A tall sycamore provided a cooling shade and sprinkled the grass around its roots with speckled bark. I glanced toward Mr. Hogan's window in the Entrance House. The shades of his office were still drawn. I could hear voices and the clop of horses in the distance, filled with the early morning energy of men who rose before the dawn to deliver milk and bread, to clean up the streets, and to wash down the sidewalks of their establishments along Ridge Avenue. The sound of such morning vitality always cheered me.

I wiped the sweat of my hands on my pants as I grabbed my shovel to take the first bite from the earth. That's when I saw the little angel sculpture, an ornamental iron cherub painted as black as the wrought-iron gates that surrounded the cemetery. The angel's face was frozen in a half smile, her chubby hand extended as if to help one who has just fallen. Her black curls hugged her head tightly. She watched me from her stone pedestal, as if patiently waiting for the grave to be dug. The tombstone, not yet placed, would bear the name *Amy Halprin*. I wondered if the angel would make good company for Amy. *Someone,* I thought, did not trust the cemetery alone to watch over their child.

I had been digging for a while when I became aware of her presence. I had a great sense for the dead, but seemed to have more difficulty with the living. I turned slowly to find a woman near my mother's age, standing alongside the dogwood tree that shaded the other side of the narrow cobblestoned driveway. I knew who she was immediately.

She was dressed in black. Her head was covered by a

long scarf that draped around her shoulders. Her blond hair spilled across her cheeks to curl beneath her chin, as if it wasn't used to such freedom. Her eyes were hollowed, as if her life had been sucked out of her, but despite that she still commanded an odd beauty.

I nodded to her, as I didn't want to break her silence. She only stared at me with an unsettling intensity.

I turned back to my task, wiping the sweat from my forehead with the back of my hand before I stepped down into the grave. I liked the smell of the damp earth. It was clean and untainted by unnatural things. I had only a few feet more to dig.

"Are you Paul?" a woman's voice asked above me. Neither curiosity or vigor fueled its tone.

I looked up to see her frowning down at me. The sycamore that rose behind her stained the sunlit sky. She shouldn't be here, I told myself. It was not right for her to watch me dig her daughter's grave.

"Yes, ma'am. I am," I replied, self-consciously leaning the shovel against the earthen wall. "How can I assist you?"

"I need you to help me find my daughter," she said matter-of-factly. "The funeral is tomorrow and I don't want to lose her." Her pale lips tightened, her face suddenly tensed with pain. I looked at the tips of her pointed black shoes and wondered how she had gotten them on today.

I felt my throat tighten. "It's too early," I said, wondering how she knew about my ability. "I can't usually connect with them until after . . . they're laid to rest. They're hard to locate now."

She narrowed her eyes as if she didn't believe me. "It will be too late," she insisted.

I didn't like her standing over me. There was something *animal* about the way she peered at me and then quickly turned her head at a far-off shout. Unlike other women I have seen, her body had a powerful presence, as if her muscles were coiled to spring in an attack.

"How did you get here?" I asked. "You really shouldn't be . . . watching this," I added.

She dismissed me with an impatient wave of her hand. "You sound like my husband," she said bitterly. "I threatened our driver if he wouldn't take me. My husband disapproves of men who like the bottle." She looked over her shoulder, in the direction of the cemetery entrance. "Where else would I be?" she demanded.

"Let me get your driver," I offered. "It's best to give yourself some time before you seek her. She'll need time to understand where she is."

I placed my palms on the ground to pull myself out of the grave. I got the tingling suspicion that she might stomp on them. But she only watched me as I dusted off and pulled at my flannel shirt to straighten it. My denim overalls were already soiled, and the brown brogans I wore looked scuffed by years of dirt. For the first time, I felt ashamed of my attire. "I will be here," I promised, before I excused myself to trot down the driveway. Mr. Hogan's window shade was thankfully up.

I burst into his office, the little bell hanging over the lintel announcing my arrival.

Mr. Hogan's bald head was bent over the counter. He was playing nervously with his handlebar mustache, something he did when he pored over his paperwork. Mr. Hogan did not think that undue excitement was proper behavior for the cemetery. As the manager of Laurel Hill, he prepared for any emotional hysteria by checking the daily burial schedule.

"Paul!" he exclaimed, his face reddening with the interruption. "What is it?"

I rubbed my mouth, surely dirtying my lips and chin. His stacks of papers extended along the length of the receptionist's counter and his own wooden desk that occupied the far corner of the room.

"The Halprin girl's mother is at her graveside. I don't feel . . . comfortable . . . with her there." Although Mr. Hogan knew of my abilities, he didn't like me to talk about them.

His mouth dropped open. "Well, that's preposterous! It is not healthy for a woman—a mother—to witness this. I will talk to her. You fetch her driver."

He nimbly ducked under the counter despite his girth. He pushed open the office door and stood on the small stone patio that was lined with planted urns. He used his hand to shield his eyes from the speckled sunlight and squinted toward the ebony angel.

"I don't see her," he said, relief in his voice.

I glanced toward the driveway entrance and noticed that her one-horse carriage was gone.

I took a deep breath. I knew she would be back tomorrow, with more desperate intentions.

———◦◦◦———

The arrival of a child or young person was always unsettling for the spirits, especially a young woman of Amy's age. Amy had been seventeen when she died. *On the cusp of becoming a woman,* I thought as I lowered myself back into her grave to trim its walls. I was a perfectionist and would not leave a fresh excavation until it was ready to seamlessly receive its coffin.

A warm breeze like a hot breath tickled my ear. I peered into the branches of the sycamore above and saw that its fertile green leaves appeared still against the blue sky. Now that Mrs. Halprin was gone, the restless spirits of Laurel Hill were making themselves known. I could feel them pressing against me. The stronger ones, like Elisha, could use their voices, or actually touch or grab me. The bruises or scratches that I sometimes bore gave testament to their frustration and fury. But the others relied on communicating by bearing down on me with a remembrance of their earthly weight.

Individually, I knew who each one was. The air they compressed carried its own unique perfume or scent— like my grandfather's pipe. But when they converged on me like a mob, I could not tell them apart. They obliterated one another's signature fragrance.

"It will be all right," I whispered into the air. "I will orient her, and you all will welcome her to ease her fear. Not all who leave the world straddling childhood and adulthood necessarily rage against their loss."

Their doubt twittered against me like butterfly wings. It was then that I felt Elisha tugging on my sleeve.

"You must beware of the mother, Paul. She'll be unlike most who seek your help. Even my own mother, God rest her soul, released me after her year of mourning." I knew he was standing close to me. The temperature of the air between us was significantly cooler.

"But this one," he continued, "seems insatiable. I can see it in her eyes."

I nodded, as I didn't want to give Elisha's words such power.

A shadow then fell across the grave, and the air around me seemed to hold its breath. Mr. Hogan was standing above me now, frowning at things he could not see.

"My boy, there are many other graves to be dug today. If you are fraternizing with the spirits, you'll need to take them with you. They must realize that they cannot be a distraction to your work."

Then he made the sign of the cross and quickly turned on his heel, taking his expansive shadow with him.

———◆———

I wasn't Mr. Hogan's only gravedigger. There were ten of us in all, but Mr. Hogan often remarked how I seemed to have a special *affinity* for the job. I was the youngest, the fastest, and preferred to work alone. The others were like

Joseph, older men who had been digging graves all their lives. Joseph, who had been working at Laurel Hill since he had arrived from Ireland thirty years ago with his wife and two lasses in tow, told me that he viewed each grave as a hole to be dug, different only from a tree pit or a privy by its coffin length. He had given up mourning for those in the coffins long ago, and had suggested that I do the same. "Otherwise the job will crush you," he said, "and all that you will look forward to is the bottle."

But I didn't feel that, at least not yet. I started at Laurel Hill at fifteen—a full year before I had communicated with my grandfather's spirit. My father, who knew Mr. Hogan through his bank, had gotten me the job. He had told Mr. Hogan that I would be a particularly sensitive and sympathetic employee—characteristics my father associated with a serious nature. Mr. Hogan liked to tell me, with a kind shake of his head, that he got more than he bargained for. "This is supposed to be a final resting place for departed souls, Paul, not a place for daily reunions." Yet he did not discourage the family or friends of the buried from seeking me out as long as they were discreet.

"She will not wish to share you," Elisha announced, suddenly by my side again as I sat on a shaded stone bench that overlooked the Schuylkill River below. It was lunchtime and I was feasting on my mother's homemade bread and strawberry jam. Before Elisha spoke, I had been listening to the hum of bees in a nearby honeysuckle bush, and breathing in the same intoxicating fragrance that beckoned them.

"Elisha, you are being harsh," I scolded. "She is simply distraught, as my mother would be." When I spoke to him or to any of the spirits, for that matter, I simply looked ahead. Below, on the River Drive, I watched two drivers pull their horses and wagons alongside each other to talk. One wagon was filled with barrels of fruits and vegetables. From my vantage point, the reds, yellows, and greens of the produce colored the wagon floor like an artist's palette. The other contained long planks of wood, cut for the construction of a house or stable.

I felt a chill on my neck, as if he had placed his hand there. "You are wrong, Paul. I've seen them before. Mothers and fathers driven mad by the loss of their child."

"But if the spirit does not wish to stay here, there is nothing they can do," I protested. Many that I had communicated with soon after their burial had simply wanted to say good-bye, to give a last warning or word of love to the ones they left behind. I learned to recognize those spirits, for our link was weak.

"But what if the spirit is raging, Paul, or is too much in love with life, like myself? If the Halprin child is in the latter category, she and her mother will keep coming back to the well until it is dry."

I nodded, shifting my weight on the bench as if making room for Elisha. He was right. I had met a pair like the ones Elisha was describing. Old Mr. Thatcher lost his thirty-year-old son, James, to a horrible fever on the brink of his wedding day. Mr. Thatcher had been planning to hand over his lumber yard to his son as a gift. When our once-a-week communications with his son—Wednesdays at dusk no matter what time of the year—were not enough, I would sometimes find him waiting for me at home on our doorstep, shaking and hollow eyed like a drunk. It was my father who forbid him to see me after that, explaining that Mr. Thatcher's fever was one that never could be broken.

It was the haunted like Mr. Thatcher that made me fear my ability.

That next morning "dawned as a funeral day," as Joseph and the other Irish liked to say. The sky was morbid with dark clouds, and by eight o'clock, remnants of last night's shadows still clung to tree branches and gathered in dark puddles beneath the tombstones and sculptures. Joseph believed that such days were fitting for a funeral, somber and respectful in their lack of brightness and life. Joseph believed that a sunny funeral day was a curse, akin to a slap in the face by God, as if the world did not suffer from the loss of this particular life....

The air was dank and stifling as was wont for June, and I sweated just from the effort of taking my place, shovel in hand, by Amy's grave. Mr. Hogan had asked that I arrive early to tidy up the area in case last night's rain had left a muddy mess around the grave site.

The grass surrounding the site was heavy with dew. Small clouds of fog blurred the air at my feet. But by the open grave, in the still soft mud, I noticed the footprints, impressions small and narrow enough to bear the weight of a child or a slight woman—like Mrs. Halprin. I felt the heaviness in my chest that I had come to recognize as a premonition of a funeral that raged against its brevity. Either the mother or the child would not accept the finality of it. I began to pat the footprints with the back of my shovel, tamping them into anonymity. As I stepped aside, I felt something hard touch my back. I cried out, despite myself, when I looked into the soulless eyes of Amy's dark angel. I wished I had talked to Mother and Father. I could have used their guidance this day.

"Can you sense her yet, Paul?" a voice called from the direction of the cobblestoned driveway. I turned from the black angel sculpture to see Mrs. Halprin standing by the curb. She was dressed in the same black dress as yesterday, but today she also wore a long black cloak that brushed against her shoes in the barest breeze. A large black hat, tied with a scarf beneath her chin, covered all her hair. Her face seemed particularly pale. The hollows beneath her eyes made them appear monstrously large in her thin face. I could see her aging driver, his shoulders hunched beneath his heavy greatcoat, standing in the open doorway to Mr. Hogan's office. Funeral attire did not recognize the seasons. The driver was waving his arms, as if defending himself from what I guessed to be Mr. Hogan's outrage at her early arrival.

I stepped away from the grave and stood beneath its sheltering sycamore.

"Is Mr. Halprin with you, ma'am? You shouldn't be here until the church ceremony is complete."

She raised her chin with contempt. Her dark eyes flashed. "He is at the church. I refused to go. It's a ridiculous waste of time."

I drew in my breath. This woman had nothing to lose. She had already denied her God and her husband.

Perhaps Elisha was right. Maybe she would be like old Mr. Thatcher, begging and at times bullying his son through me to find a way back into the world.

"Mrs. Halprin, why don't you let me take you to the office? You can rest there comfortably as you wait for the funeral party. You'll get weak in this smothering air." I prayed I sounded dispassionate, despite my thumping heart. As long as her gaze rested on my face, I felt a terrible unease.

She smiled, not unkindly. "You must call me Jenny, as we will probably come to be good friends."

I froze for a moment, until I found my tongue. "I couldn't do that, Mrs. Halprin. It would not be...proper," I finished lamely.

"As if I am?" she asked, arching her brows.

I wanted to yell for Mr. Hogan and was relieved to see him barreling out of his office, as he pulled his watch out of his shirt pocket and frowned at the time. As he marched toward us along the cobblestoned driveway, he turned to throw a withering look at Mrs. Halprin's poor driver, who by this time was sitting on the ornamental iron bench beneath the office window. He was dabbing at his forehead with a handkerchief.

"Mrs. Halprin," Mr. Hogan began. I could hear the

tension in his voice as he strained to contain his horror. "You must not dally around the grave site. It is most unusual and of no comfort to you and your family. You must trust me in this."

Again she raised her eyebrows, as if skeptical of his assessment. She pulled at the fingertips of her black gloves as if she toyed with the idea of pulling them off and slapping him across the face.

"Has my husband not paid for the grave, sir?" she asked coldly. She glanced my way as if to gauge my reaction. I could not help but look toward Mr. Hogan. Death and its accompanying rituals were somber, and all affected had an expected role to play. Women particularly, after their initial anticipated hysteria, were expected to fade back from life and mourn the death of a husband or child for a year, sometimes two. Mrs. Halprin's impudence was an abomination.

Mr. Hogan's chin dropped and he stuttered for a moment. "My dear lady," he said when he found his voice. "It is not a question of payment, but a question of respect and observance of the ceremony." He adjusted his spectacles over his full, flushed cheeks. "As the director of Laurel Hill, I would not be doing my duty if I allowed you to endanger yourself. Many a mourner has suffered from prolonged hysteria after the loss of a family member. For you to dwell here can take you too close to that abyss."

Mr. Hogan had his arms crossed now, resting them on his ample stomach. When it came to matters of the protocol of the cemetery, Mr. Hogan rarely lost an argument.

"Very well, then," Mrs. Halprin sniffed. "I will accompany Paul as he performs his ground duties until my daughter arrives."

Mrs. Halprin was true to her word, much to my chagrin. She followed me like a late afternoon shadow, lagging behind by just a few yards, but seemingly tethered to me by the thin, dark premonition of our connection. The funeral was still an hour or so away, I realized with a good degree of discomfort. I felt the ball of panic in me tighten as I watched Mr. Hogan turn on his heels and throw his hands up in the air in incredulous defeat.

Mrs. Halprin redirected her hallowed-eyed stare at me. "Well, Paul, whom must you tend to next?" she asked. "I wouldn't mind leaving Amy's...site...for a little while."

I did have some tending that I needed to do, but most of that work was for the newly interred. The work at these graves was always the same—removing the mounds of now disintegrating bouquets and mementos that symbolized the pain and frenzy behind a new loss, before the saving transition to a more respectful, calm remembrance of the dead. But I was afraid to take Mrs. Halprin to any of these sites. Their spirits were still raw in the grave, and they sometimes clung to my ankles if I came too close, trying to draw me down to them. But I soon learned that this action was a remnant of their shock and confusion. They simply wanted confirmation of where they were and how their loved ones fared. Most often, after their first encounter with me, they settled in and moved on. But Mrs. Halprin's separation from Amy was fresh. I couldn't take the chance of some recalcitrant spirit latching on to her. Some of the new ones might immediately sense her desperation. They would cling to her like a cobweb, encouraged by her yearning to be close to the dead.

It was then I decided that it was time to tend Elisha's mausoleum.

We followed the cobblestoned driveway to the highest bluff, which overlooked the Schuylkill River, as I did not wish to cut across any restless grave sites. I picked up my shovel and distractedly allowed it to drop and clang against the driveway stone, doing my best to submit all of my attention to the tepid raindrops that tipped from the leaves above us to hit our cheeks or splotch our clothes. I felt the distraction would be a welcome relief from the life-strangling air.

"Are you going to continue with that racquet until we wake all the dead?" Mrs. Halprin asked.

"The dead do not need to be wakened," I said nervously, then immediately regretted my honest response.

She grabbed my shoulder, forcing me to come to a stop.

"How do you know them so well?" she asked. The sarcasm was gone from her voice.

I turned to look into her face and this time truly allowed myself to see her. Suddenly she seemed vulnerable like a child. She wore no rouge or powder, and the fine lines in her face were ageless marks of anguish. Her blue eyes were soft and beseeching. She tilted her chin up at me expectantly. What could I say, I wondered, for I did not understand it all myself.

Behind Mrs. Halprin, the stone markers of the dead sprouted from the descending hillside like symbols of surrender. Time or disease had eventually won, yet not all those buried beneath the monuments their loved ones erected to insist on their memory were quite ready to give up. How *did* I know this?

"I'm not sure," I replied, knowing it was not the

response she wanted to hear. Her eyes clouded, and she allowed her hand to drop to her side.

"My parents could probably explain it. They have been spiritualists for a long time. I only... sense it," I added, more in a whisper.

She gave me a wary smile. "Then I need you to explain what you can."

I looked up toward the heavens, which seemed particularly weighed down today with clouds puffed up with dark anger or dread. They appeared so low that I felt I might touch them.

"I feel a connection," I said, glancing at the gravestones surrounding us. "At first, it was more of a sense that it was impossible. Impossible that people who lived with such vigor and passion could so easily be snuffed out from the world."

Her eyes were eager now, bright with anticipation. This time she clasped my free hand with hers.

"You do not believe in an afterlife?" she asked.

I knew that the answer to that question meant everything to her.

"Yes, I do. Of course," I insisted. "But I also believe that the... energies of people... somehow survive, like a coal that has been extinguished yet still glows with the heat it remembers," I struggled to explain. "It's that energy, and its necessity to wean itself from this world, that keeps the spirits of some people among us for a while."

"Just a while?" she asked sharply. Again I knew the answer she wanted, but I did not wish to give her false hope.

"For most, it's not long. Some pass right through." I surveyed the hundreds of graves in our immediate vicinity. Of those, perhaps there were ten that I knew whose spirits were still present in some way. "Usually, it's those who feel that their work was not done or that something that was extremely important to them was unresolved. They're the ones that linger."

But Amy was just a young woman. Her life had barely begun, I reminded myself.

"For children, the passing is sometimes like a tantrum," I attempted to explain. "Their most precious gift had been taken abruptly away from them. But young people, on the threshold of maturity, and especially young women, are prone to melancholy and willing to release life as if it were a bad dream."

She turned away from me as if she anticipated a blow.

"Can I take you back to the office, Mrs. Halprin? Forgive me, I didn't mean to upset you."

I recoiled at my own indiscretion. I had never spoken so bluntly to anyone but my parents in such a way.

But Mrs. Halprin turned slowly back to me. Her eyes were narrowed in a squint.

"Don't be ridiculous, Paul. I mean to stay with you until Amy arrives."

We exchanged no words for some time. She seemed content to stand along the driveway curb. I could feel her stare on my back as I picked my way among the grave sites, pulling some weeds or tidying bouquets that had been scattered by the winds and rain. I was afraid to do anything to the graves themselves. I didn't want to provoke anxiety over her own daughter's final resting place. I wanted her to see how we cared for our residents, staying away from the resting places of those who did not yet completely rest.

All with the exception of Elisha. As we made our way to the top of the hill, his mausoleum loomed before us. Elisha was standing in front of his austere stone structure. His home for forty some years now. His arms were folded.

"Get rid of her, Paul. She is poison." He stared at her as if looking out over the bow of a ship into the horror of an impending Arctic storm.

"This one is with you, isn't he?" she asked, tilting her head toward the mausoleum, trembling.

Mrs. Halprin knew by the shock on my face that she was right.

"How can you say that?" I demanded of Elisha in a hissed whisper. "She is in mourning, man!"

"Are you speaking to him?" she asked, her face animated by a nervous excitement. She reached out to clutch my arm.

"It is nothing. I often talk to myself amid the monuments." I knew it was useless to lie, particularly since I had already told her of my gift, but Elisha was almost frantic.

"She is a life-sucker, boy—a vampire in the truest sense. I have met a number of her kind during my time in the world. They are the walking dead—living beings who consume the life energies of others."

I turned to appraise Mrs. Halprin, who now had an odd, elated smile on her face. She looked nothing like the monster Elisha described. Her black scarf was pulled tightly about her face, exaggerating its oval form. Her blue eyes were bright—maybe a bit delirious. She stood rock still, straining to hear or see whatever I was communicating with.

A soft, wet breeze pushed at the air, causing the dew-laden blades of grass to shudder. I could smell the heavy fragrance of her rose-scented perfume, a scent unlike those of the roving cemetery spirits.

"Who is he?" she asked. "What is he saying?" She then glanced at the name the mausoleum bore over its ornate entrance.

"Elisha Kent Kane," she said to herself in awe.

"Do you know of him?" I asked, desperate to make our conversation normal.

"Know of him? Of course! I would be a recluse not to have heard of the heroic North Pole adventures of Dr. Kane." Her tone sounded suddenly mocking.

I looked at Elisha, who was now pacing furiously. He scowled at her. His eyes narrowed beneath his bushy brows.

"You must get her out of here, Paul," he warned ominously.

"She is here for her daughter's funeral," I argued, no longer concerned with upholding our charade.

"Then take her to her daughter's grave, so that she can devour the spirit of her own progeny." Elisha's voice was laced with venom.

I was speechless. I had never heard such violence from Elisha, such obvious abhorrence for the spirit of the still living.

"What is it about her that makes you say such things?" I asked. For now, I truly needed to know. A disturbing fear had been gnawing at me about Mrs. Halprin. Elisha's reaction to her only fed those fears.

"Does he dislike me, Paul?" She moved closer to the mausoleum, and reached her hand out as if to stroke its smooth, white-stone wall.

Elisha immediately placed himself between Mrs. Halprin and the structure. She stopped, as if sensing his presence there.

She then shivered and pulled at her black cloak. Her smile matured into one of full knowledge.

"Of course not, Mrs. Halprin," I rushed to insist. "The spirits are sensitive to . . . a sudden loss of the living. Such a loss churns up memories of their own loved ones." I threw Elisha a threatening look. "Why don't we continue to the terrace overlooking the river? It is a peaceful, inspiring spot."

"The river?" she echoed. "Does it calm you because it is ageless, because it can never die?"

I wouldn't have known what to say, but I didn't have a chance to scramble for a response, as we were interrupted by the plaintive wails of the funeral dirge that plied the air, rising from the bowl of the entrance. I didn't have to see it. They all were the same. Black bunted carriages pulled by horses festooned with ebony ribbons plodded along the driveway, the funeral carriage already pulled to the side of the grave. Women in black dresses, capes, and hats—for none dared to wear color that signified life—were helped from the carriage by the gentlemen who accompanied them. The men, whose morning coats and homburgs were always black, wore matching armbands. Their somber cries or words swelled like an orchestra, gaining strength as each carriage emptied its occupants.

I knew Amy's funeral hearse had arrived.

"Thank God," Elisha proclaimed. "Take her to her own table."

Mrs. Halprin stiffened. The smile was gone from her face. A veiled anger had replaced it.

"Come, Mrs. Halprin. I will escort you down and assist in any way I can," I offered. I couldn't help but look at Elisha. Where did such loathing come from? And how was I to discover its source?

"I expect nothing less from you, Paul." Her hand reached out to squeeze my own. The gentleness of her touch belied the steel in her voice.

Mrs. Halprin was enraged by her husband's presence. He was playing his part in the funeral and did not have any other expectations. She made a sound as if she were sucking in air when he snapped his fingers at her, an implied order to stand by his side. Mr. Hogan, in one of his many black mourning suits, waved his arms, his means of providing *discreet* direction to Joseph to tie up the horses and hearse. He grabbed the funeral guests by their elbows, placing them alongside the grave as if each had a practiced part in this service. Mrs. Halprin glanced at him dismissively.

The sky had colored to a darker shade. A second wave of storms was perilously evident. The damp, blackened limbs of the trees were suddenly buoyant, uplifted by gusts of warm air. The white tombstones were gray beneath the bare-limbed trees and miserly light. The grass seemed to tremble at the breath of the coming storm.

I looked toward Amy's black angel. She alone remained unperturbed.

"Make her leave me alone . . . ," a young woman's voice called to me. "I wish to be left alone."

Amy! Hearing her voice struck me like a lightning bolt. It was too early for her to protest against the living's desire to intervene. And it was certainly too early for me to try to reason with her. "You must make her stop," she pleaded. "She cannot be allowed to pursue me into death!"

Hush, I thought, begging her to be still, although I knew no one else could hear me. *Give your mother time*, I implored.

But Amy, on the brink of being interred, would hear none of it.

"She knows nothing of time. She respects no natural laws," she insisted. "It is your job to keep her from me. I have sacrificed everything for this!" Her outrage pounded inside my head.

I didn't dare to tell her, at this moment, that my job was to bring spirits and people together.

Mrs. Halprin was staring at me. I didn't know how much my face revealed. Such early communication at the graveside had never occurred.

Did you invite death? I thought, hoping that her reply would confirm how preposterous and appalling my question was.

"You are a spiritualist!" was her angry reply. "Need I lend a false respect to your question?"

Before I could answer, I sensed her spirit withdraw, tumultuous as a tantrum, to a place that I could not reach. The spirits of Laurel Hill told me they called this place they took refuge in "the garden." The place that the living could not reach them through pleas and prayers. The place that offered them a temporary tranquility. Even spiritual-ists such as I were kept outside of the garden's gates, as it was a respite from humanity's relentless quest for answers about the afterlife. The spirits insisted that it was a relief to them when those who knew them died. Only then were they truly free from the demands of the living. Love and loyalty forged during life transcended earthbound ties. Only death could relinquish the final ledgers of living.

"How does one get to the garden?" I once asked, thinking along non corporeal terms. A spirit was a spirit no matter where one was located, it seemed to me.

"It is unexplainable," was the agreed-upon answer. "Even the heart is stilled there to barely a beat. It is the closest to dust that we can become before we move on to the other."

I had thought that a sad thing.

I straightened when I noticed Mrs. Halprin was star-ing at me from the rim of the grave. She knew something was going on.

I looked at the other funeral participants clustered close to one another in fear of death or a greater force. Blurs of soft golden light outlined their forms. I could see this in all living beings when they gathered in close quar-ters, and around the presence of more powerful spirits like

Elisha. Usually I found this comforting, but Amy's shattering of our boundary so prematurely had left me shaken.

I looked for Elisha and saw him by the carriage. What was he doing, standing with his arms crossed and staring at Mrs. Halprin as she clung to her husband's arm, who was transfixed as the pallbearers lowered Amy's coffin into the grave. It was the first time I had seen her look truly stricken.

Suddenly I could feel the burnished edges of the coffin as the men gently slackened the rope. Feel it as if I were the body that lay inside. I was keenly aware of the cool, freshly dug earthen walls and could see the tiny strands of roots that had been laid bare when I carved out this grave. I experienced this sensation with every one I dug. This was the only trait my parents could never explain.

Do you understand, Amy? I asked, attempting to draw her back safely to the world. It was hard for me not knowing when she might return from the garden, her fury for her mother fresh as life. As a soldier knows the form and smells of his earthen trenches, we know the dimensions and taste of our subsurface enclosure. Both provided a sense of safety, the one certainly was more permanent. *It will get easier,* I promised.

"Let us pray," the minister began, obviously in some distress. He clutched his Bible as he said the prayers. I didn't know if it was the roiling that he sensed in Mrs. Halprin or a natural empathy at having to be the one to preside over the service of one so young.

He gently continued, draining the sorrow from his voice, fearing the hysteria it might cause. Those gathered closest to the minister and the Halprins glanced furtively at one another with some suspicion. Men in black top hats and women in black dresses that trembled against the ground at the whisper of each tepid breeze appeared to be holding their breath.

That is when Mrs. Halprin screamed. A scream of such inconsolable grief that it jolted every man, woman, and child. "A cry of the banshee," Joseph would later say when telling the story to his crew, recalling the female spirits from his homeland whose terror-inducing wailings warned of imminent death. Her husband recoiled as she balled her gloved fists in front of her mouth.

All were riveted to their spots as she wailed, until one by one, they released their own cries of grief. The crushing wave of hopelessness that Mrs. Halprin had unleashed elicited its own communal response. Those who had been the most stoic or nervous as they stood by the grave had been granted permission to cry out against the heavens for all imaginable injustices against life. And I, who had expected to see shock and horror on the faces of Mrs. Halprin's acquaintances at her petrifying keen, saw an assembly of the grief-stricken, who only needed one parent's permission to cry out their own fears.

A gentleman to my left, still quite young as the soft fuzz of hair above his lip and on his chin marked his age like the still smooth bark of a tree, gripped my shoulder with ferocity. But as he was not close enough to it, I could not tell him death's grip on those who have passed from this world was a much gentler one.

What truly unnerved me was the effect that such an explosion of protest might have on Amy's delicate, ethereal state, particularly if she were bitter about her life. Many restless spirits remarked on how the living cared so generously for them only after their demise. I thought of going to Mrs. Halprin, to grab her hands to bring her back into her sad reality.

That is when Elisha distracted me. He was standing behind the carriage horses and I was sure he was whispering into their ears one of his horrendous tales of the Arctic. The horses' eyes were wild, their nostrils flared. They jerked their heads in a desperation to flee.

And thus they were off, the carriage pounded and swayed over the cobblestones, straight through Elisha, as the horses trampled toward the cemetery exit.

A number of people gaped and pulled their Bibles to their breasts. Mr. Hogan began shouting for Joseph and the crew. The minister, still in shock at the depth of Mrs. Halprin's despair, stumbled a foot or two away from the grave. Mr. Halprin frowned, but with a relief at being able to turn away from his wife, who had stopped screaming finally, silenced by the commotion of the horses. Indeed, the scream was now replaced with the barest hint of a patronizing smile, a smile that said to me that she recognized her daughter's handiwork in all things.

That smile contained more than I could ever understand at the time. Beneath its benign appearance, I later learned it held more power and single-mindedness than I had ever encountered in another living being. Its sole purpose was to bring back the dead. I, despite my youth and ability to speak with the spirits, knew the impossibility and tragedy behind such a quest. But I could not have fathomed the misguided confidence and false righteousness that powered its existence. The remaining few weeks that I shared with Mrs. Halprin should have told me much about her and her ubiquitous smile, but my strength, to my downfall, was never in understanding the living.

She came to the cemetery every day. I often found her waiting for me at the entrance gate in her carriage, her driver hunched miserably on his seat, holding the reins in his hands as if they were something blasphemous.

And Mr. Hogan, much to his frustration, could do nothing about it. Her daughter was buried here in one of the most popular sites in the cemetery. The black angel, whom he couldn't help but view from his office window, was a daily haunting reminder.

Her visits were predictable and precise. She arrived before dawn, dressed as if she were attending a tea party or a ladies' club. She wore summer frocks, refusing to wear black after the funeral, for she told me she expected Amy "to be back." Her blond hair was pinned up in a youthful way, rebellious strands clinging to her neck in the heat. Her face still held the disturbing presence of a sly young girl when she seemed unaware of one's glance her way.

She scandalized all who saw her. She drove Mr. Hogan to such desperate lengths that he purchased a woman's mourning dress and kept it in his office closet, in hopes that the insanity that inhabited her mind would suddenly vacate. Mr. Hogan was never given the opportunity to release the black garment from his closet.

Her husband joined her periodically, and only on those days did she wear her mourning dress and veil. *She* may have sensed a divine intervention that told her that her daughter still walked among us, but she could not convince her husband of it.

They both appeared petulant during their visits, and Mrs. Halprin was not allowed to follow me as I conducted my tasks. Those were the good days for us. Joseph and his crew were unnerved by the woman they continued to call "the banshee." "She can bring nothing but bad fortune upon us," Joseph insisted.

One morning, standing by Amy's grave, I asked Mrs. Halprin if her husband believed in spiritualism, whether or not he, too, was hoping to communicate with his daughter.

She barked a cruel laugh. "He only comes here to keep up appearances. He didn't care about Amy. I believe he actually resented her because she was the sole owner of my affection." She looked at me, expecting my protest. When I said nothing, she added, "He is a heartless man."

"I can't believe that, Mrs. Halprin," I replied, bending to pull at the roots of the dandelion weeds that were beginning to wander onto Amy's still raw grave. The tang of the rich earth stung my nostrils and I winced, carrying the annoyance into my tone with Mrs. Halprin. "He was her father. His love is bound to be different from your own, but no less in value."

But it was her mother that Amy wasn't fond of. Or at the least, her spirit seemed immune to her mother's pleas. When I reached out to her, with her mother at my side, I heard or felt nothing, as if death had completely swallowed her spirit.

When I shared this with Elisha, he seemed to think for a few moments, before he nodded to himself to add, "It was the girl herself who spooked the funeral horses, not me. It seems she will do whatever she can to rid herself of her mother. Haven't you noticed, boy?" he asked. "Every vibrant spirit in this cemetery hides in its deepest corners when that woman is here. The spirits know what she is."

He was right. It was eerily quiet when Mrs. Halprin dogged my shadow. Nothing tickled my consciousness or reached for my arms or legs in pleading. Each spirit had simply reconciled with its fate. Only Elisha felt strong enough to fend off her hunger. But when *I* looked at her, I only saw a grieving mother who refused to believe in death.

After a few weeks I had grown weary of escorting Mrs. Halprin about the cemetery. Her presence was heavier than the July air, fat with its drenching moisture. With her by my side, I felt trapped in a bell jar that contained my movements and cut me off from all communications with the spirit world. I continued my daily chores at the cemetery—help dig the graves, tidy the earthen mounds, and plant and tend the flowers that would bring some color to the interminably gray world that greeted the bereaved. On that last summer night, a night full of stars and the smell of the lethargically flowing Schuylkill River, I stayed past our closing time and vowed to talk to Amy.

Mr. Hogan had been locking up his office when he turned, by instinct, to see me sitting cross-legged by Amy's grave. I was leaning against the pedestal of the black angel, thinking of exactly how I would appeal to Amy to advise her mother to stay away from the cemetery—that her future with her daughter would require at least a few more decades or an earlier demise. I was nervous about broaching this subject, for I knew by now that Amy did indeed despise her mother, as she scolded me with fury after each of Mrs. Halprin's visits. I didn't want her here either, but I also did not want her destroyed. I simply wanted her to give me, and the other spirits that still

roamed the cemetery grounds, the freedom to be our-
selves again.

"What are you doing, Paul?" Mr. Hogan asked suspi-
ciously. His eyes squinted whenever he looked at the
angel. It was more respectable—and safer—for Mr. Hogan
to dislike a sculpture.

"I have a bit more . . . tending to do, sir," I answered
evasively. He tolerated, even encouraged, my communicating with the dead, knowing I had a settling effect on
them and could calm their initial terrors. But I knew he
would not approve of any spiritual dealings that involved
Mrs. Halprin.

"It will be dark in an hour," he said, although a July
twilight often glowed well past nine. "You know I don't
want you here after dark." He tugged at his shirtsleeves,
uncomfortable in the still sweltering heat. Sweat shone on
his neck and forehead, and a damp shadow stained his
shirt below his collar. I smiled at him, despite myself.
Daily we were surrounded by the graves, obelisks, and
other monuments of the dead, yet he still feared the dark
for me.

"Why are you smiling, Paul?" he asked, his eyes
acquiring a mischievous brightness. He placed one large
hand against a marble pillar as he pulled his handkerchief

from his jacket pocket to dab at his face. "Are you making light of my concerns? Just because you hobnob with spirits doesn't mean that you should be free of our normal apprehension about death."

"No, no, of course not, Mr. Hogan," I rushed to assure him, standing to block his view of the angel. "But we do spend most of our waking hours here. Darkness, compared to death, seems like a sheltering friend. It hides most things that would frighten us."

"I know that nothing in the cemetery frightens you, Paul," He sighed. "We all should be so blessed. I just wish to ensure that that part of you never changes."

"I will be cautious with the girl, Mr. Hogan. You and I know that it must be done, and now is the time to do it." The momentary silence between us was filled with the drowsy thrums of the cicadas.

"I can stay with you, Paul, just to keep you company," he offered. He glanced around to confirm that Mrs. Halprin was not hiding behind one of the many tombstones that crowded her daughter's grave.

"That is not necessary, sir. You should get home to your wife and daughter. My parents know that I will be working a little late tonight. They intend to come for me by carriage at ten o'clock. They trust me with this."

"Then, by all means, Paul, I trust you, too—trust that you will care for your own safety." I nodded as he turned away. He then said, without turning back, "Tell the girl to give her mother peace in whatever way she can. It is what we all wish for."

It wasn't long before I felt the presence of Amy behind my left shoulder. I remember thinking how odd it was that the energy of her spirit was so concentrated, like an orb that I could place my hands around. Elisha's energies were diffuse, as if his spirit were dissected by the rays of sunlight that lit his days. I realized only later, when I myself had crossed over, that the forms of such energies were dependent on one's years on earth. Experience and life unwound the tightly spun threads of the soul.

"I will not allow this," she said, a petulance in her tone that confirmed her youth. "I did not purposely leave this world to be pursued by my mother in the afterlife. She smothered me on earth and now intends to smother me in my grave?"

She was shouting in a silent, horrifying fashion that only tortured spirits can attain. The hum of the cicadas swelled as if in competition and the tombstones in our immediate area began to glow like gaslight. I had never experienced such a thing.

Amy herself was a new attraction. Her anger at the living seemed to strike a long dormant chord in her neighbors. Like the living, the spirits can be rallied when they recognize common ground.

I turned to face what I sensed, and cried out and stumbled into the outstretched hand of the black angel. Amy was standing there in full body—a shimmering, glowing shadow of the girl who stood beside her mother only weeks ago.

She was slight and appeared more childish in her bed-clothes. Her hair was loose around her shoulders. Ribbons, encircling strands on each side of her forehead, cascaded against her cheeks. Her face was thin, her bone structure high and fine. The sheer sleeves of her sleeping gown exposed tiny wrists and knobby elbows. Yet her face contained a beauty beyond her seventeen years. I knew she was not buried in such a wardrobe. *Is this how Amy feels comfortable? Or was this another rebuke aimed at her mother?*

"My mother would not have approved," she answered my unspoken thought. The first hint of a self-satisfied smile touched her face.

"You are so young to harbor such anger," I stammered, shielding my eyes against the intensity of her light. It was as if her grave site were being visited by the sun at high noon when the rest of the cemetery had to settle for twilight. "What could she have done to cause your soul to burn like a bonfire?" I asked.

Amy tossed her ribboned hair over her shoulders with a flick of her hand. She narrowed her eyes and shut her thoughts from me.

"From her mother's own mold," a voice whispered in my ear. I spun around to see Elisha only a few feet away, his hands poised on the top of equally high tombstones as if he were swinging open a gate. His ice-crusted beard jiggled gently with his laughter.

"What do you know about any of this?" Amy demanded, lured back by the taunting. She rested her hands on her hips and eyed Elisha like hired help.

"Nothing," He laughed. "Except that you need to calm down, dearie, and free us all from the wrath you hold for your mother."

Suddenly Elisha became serious and approached us with the careful, expansive steps that his snow boots required. "Paul is one of the living that tends to us, and he does so with a wisdom that is unmatched by any living being more than four times his age. Your mother is a distraction. A burden to his spiritual senses."

I wanted to say something, but I was silenced by

Elisha's stern stare. He paused to allow Amy to speak.

She seemed suspicious and raised her chin to meet Elisha's haughty gaze. "And what about you and the . . . others?" she asked. "Am I a distraction to them, also?"

There was a quiver in her voice, which Elisha must have noticed, for his look and his tone softened.

"My dear child," he replied. "Look." As he made this recommendation, he swung his large, gloved hand to encompass the cemetery around us. I believe Amy gasped along with me as we both stared at the shimmering forms that stood by the hundreds of gravestones that fanned across the cemetery hillside. It was as if Mr. Hogan had the cemetery crew post a lantern upon the stones still harboring our active spirits. Their features were not clear, nor were they as bright as Amy, yet a column of concentrated light stood sentinel by many grave sites—waiting and watching for the settling of her spirit.

"They see you like a wild colt—not such a bad thing if your death had been a tragedy."

"But it was a tragedy," I interrupted, despite my shock at our phantomlike audience. She wasn't just a spoiled girl, as Elisha was implying. She was a beautiful young woman on the cusp of freedom, who took her own life. I saw pain in her petulance.

"Why did you do it?" I whispered. I could feel Elisha's curiosity like a hand on my shoulder. One like Elisha who had roared in and out of life could never understand a willing relinquishing of it.

Amy looked down, pulling her arms across her chest as if to hold on to herself. She let out a long whimper before she finally replied.

"My mother stifled me because she gave up on her own life long ago. She lived her lost life through mine." Amy bit her lip, as if confronted by a terrible realization. "I did it to finally get away from her. I couldn't imagine decades of her touching my clothes, sniffing at my friends, refusing to allow me to go to the market or any place unescorted. She clung to me with a forcefulness that made me despise her touch and the sound of her voice. I wanted to make her stop."

"There were better ways to do that, dearie, for complaints so common between mothers and daughters," Elisha said without sarcasm.

I looked at him crossly but he paid me no mind.

Amy's hand went to her throat. She tugged at something that lay beneath her collar. She slowly pulled a heart-shaped golden locket from her sleeping gown.

"Ah, you had a suitor," Elisha said with approval.

"He might have been," Amy whispered, staring vacantly into the present that dashed all hope of the past.

Had the suitor broken Amy's heart? But then why was her anger directed at her mother? It didn't make sense.

I turned to Amy. "I am sorry I didn't know you in life, Amy. But I am here to help you now, in this life," I offered.

This time she looked at me directly. Her eyes were full.

"Tonight, Paul, I will continue to wail and rage at my stupidity, as Dr. Kane so politely avoided naming when addressing my rashness. My neighbors will have to bear with me for just a bit longer." She gave a shy nod to all the shimmering forms that made themselves visible, stunned by or in awe of her.

"Tomorrow, through you, I will speak to my mother," she added, "to gain her promise that she will leave us all in peace."

Despite myself, I still did not want to see Mrs. Halprin devastated.

"You will be kind, Amy, as she truly loves you despite her ways?" I asked.

"Did she?" Elisha questioned. "Amy appears to be of another opinion."

But Amy only nodded. "This will be my gift from the grave to her."

I had purposely avoided Mrs. Halprin that morning. Her carriage arrived at the same time it always did, during the timid light following dawn. But this time I was by Elisha's mausoleum, enjoying the view of the river plied by the day's first ferries. I had busied myself for at least an hour there, until the sky acquired a clarity usually reserved for the fall. I took a deep breath and was heartened, as if a great burden had already been lifted. Mrs. Halprin would have been by Amy's grave by now and if Amy was fulfilling her promise to us, she would call to me soon. Mrs. Halprin's daily visits should come to a close.

"Elisha," I called. "Should you wander over there . . . to make sure that Amy is all right?" I expected to hear from her by now.

I avoided the urge to turn and make my way down the cobblestoned roadway to catch a glimpse of Mrs. Halprin. I realized that I was afraid . . . for Amy . . . and for what might happen.

"You know better than that," Elisha protested over my shoulder. "No living or deceased entity wants interference during such delicate moments."

"But I feel that this time is different, Elisha. Both the living and the dead are in turmoil in the Halprin family.

The intensity of their feelings makes me uneasy." I didn't need to explain to Elisha. He read my anxieties like his trusted compass.

"Nonsense, Paul," he chided, stepping in front of me to command my full attention. His blue eyes were stern beneath his bushy brows. His burnished nose and crusted beard reminded me that Elisha spoke from a particularly harsh and frigid place. Elisha's Arctic past had blasted away all squanderous sentimentality. "Do you not have a job to do at this moment?" he asked. "She will summon you when she is ready."

I nodded. I was to prepare a grave before noon at the softly greened terrace site just south of Elisha's mausoleum.

I picked up my shovel and left Elisha, feeling his presence weaken as I made my way to the new site. He was right, of course, I told myself, allowing the silent white stones that marked each individual memory to fill my vision. Only here did the man-made memorials to the dead coexist peacefully with the living.

I looked in the direction of Amy's grave, which was downslope and hidden by trees and the curve of the hill. Instead I saw Joseph and two of his assistants propping their shovels against the trunk of a large sycamore that leaned over a family plot, separated from the open space by a waist-high iron railing. A funeral was planned for three children from this family who died from the typhoid. Its recent reappearance had kept Joseph and his crew busy these past weeks.

Joseph tipped his hat and waved. The other two men, younger than he and still brawny about their arms with their shirtsleeves rolled up, did the same. Although Joseph was kind and friendly to me, I knew he preferred to work with the Irish from his own neighborhood, who shared his beliefs about the dead. They did not fear me, but they did not know how to accept my ability to attract the spirits. I returned the wave and continued on. I was looking forward to time alone.

When I reached the spot, I couldn't help but draw in my breath at the beauty of the view here, a beauty that defied time and the significance of man. The deciduous and evergreen trees that crowded this hillside before it plunged toward the now swiftly flowing river provided a sturdy company for the newly departed destined for these plots. And the river, like these spirits, was eternal.

The spot that I was to dig was marked with rope and I felt the ease of the shovel through the moist, rough soil from my boot to my shoulder. The earth felt so welcoming that I didn't initially notice the heat of the sun on my back or the buzz of the gnats that did battle about my ears. I tried to keep my thoughts on the new person that would inhabit this grave as I kept my rhythm with the shovel, despite the sweat that soon clung to my forehead and neck.

"I told you to stay away from me," Amy scolded.

I froze as my shovel hit the earth. The stone particles in the newly exposed earth shimmered in the sun. Although I wasn't standing by Amy's grave, she knew that I could still be her medium. Elisha said that my ability to hear the dead hawked itself like a spectral flare. At first, I thought she was talking to me.

"Your sorrow means nothing to me now." Amy's tone was harsh—anger coiled around each word like the ribbons in her hair. "You traced my steps like a pathetic shadow—if not literally, then through your questions and taunts. You were jealous of me!" she cried.

I realized then that she wasn't addressing me. She was talking to Mrs. Halprin.

"I cannot say these things to your mother. Not now," I pleaded. "She's freshly mourning." I closed my eyes and grasped my shovel, hoping to channel my conviction to Amy. Surely I could convince her. Instead, an image of Amy flashed through my mind. She stood in her nightclothes, arms crossed, her face grim and immovable. The hair that fell about her shoulders suddenly turned to fire.

"She betrayed me!" she spat. And suddenly, I saw in my mind a grainy image, as if I were peering through a window into a room not yet lit against the dying light. Mrs. Halprin was holding a tall young man in her arms. I could see that he was young by his coltish stance. His head rested on Mrs. Halprin's shoulder.

"You'll have heatstroke, Paul." A woman's voice knocked me from my reverie.

"Mrs. Halprin," I exclaimed, freezing in mid-stroke watching her descend the set of stone stairs that had been dug into the hillside for visitors to the terrace. As usual, her hair was pulled back into a chignon. She wore a cream-colored dress that caught the anemic breeze with its hem. She was holding one of the white enamel cups that Mr. Hogan kept by the watering spigot outside of his office. She offered it to me, a sad smile on her face.

"You work so hard. I brought you some water. I wanted to do one act of kindness for you before I said good-bye."

I hesitated. I didn't know what to say. My hands gripped the handle of the shovel as if it were railing.

"Please, it's the least I can do for you, particularly as

this is my last visit . . . at least for some time," she said. Her tone was strangely cautious.

"Thank you, Mrs. Halprin." I searched her face as I accepted the cup for some sign that she had overheard me. But her face was oddly calm and the water felt good against my parched throat.

"Thank you," I said, resisting the urge to wipe my mouth with my forearm. Instead, I placed the cup on the grass near the steps, so that I wouldn't forget to return it to the office.

"Is everything all right?" I asked.

She stood on the bottom step, only a few yards away from the grave I was digging. I then noticed the slightest tremor in her hand as she reached to push back a loose strand of hair from her forehead.

"Amy spoke to you," she replied. "Obviously she doesn't wish to speak to me." Her blue eyes suddenly hardened, yet flashed a new vulnerability. "Did Amy tell you about Thomas?" she asked, probing me with her eyes searching for a visible answer. Her voice abandoned its control. It was suddenly accusing.

I pulled my handkerchief from my back pocket and wiped my forehead. I swatted at the whining gnat close to my ear.

"She suggested to me that she had a suitor in her life, but she didn't call him by name," I answered. I looked longingly at the earth, to the place where my shovel now rested. I could do no more for Mrs. Halprin.

"Did she tell you that I stole Thomas away from her? That I invited him to our home when I was alone?" she demanded. Her voice was suddenly shrill.

"I did it for Amy. I did everything for Amy!" she insisted. "He obviously wasn't good enough for her, as he was all too willing to keep personal company with her mother. It's all I could have done!" she screamed.

I didn't want to hear more. She had said enough for me to understand the depth of Amy's despair.

"She will forgive you in time," I said softly.

"By mocking my visits to this cemetery? She does not want my company. She will be alone here!" she cried.

"No. That is where you are wrong, Mrs. Halprin. She will find her place among the spirits in the cemetery and will move on when she is ready. I can help her with that." Again she gave me an odd, fleeting smile, devoid of any context. She grabbed at my arm and held on to it, as if desperate for me to understand.

"Thomas did not deserve Amy. She knows that now," she asserted.

"Let me take you to the office, Mrs. Halprin. Mr. Hogan will have you rest there before your journey home," I said as I gently pulled away from her. Her hand dropped lifelessly to her side.

"That is not necessary, Paul." She waved me off. "I came here to say good-bye to you, and to ask that you promise to keep Amy company." Her gaze moved to the cup lying in the grass. "Give that to me, dear. I'll be ready for a cup of water myself by the time I walk back to the office."

"Of course," I said, barely feeling guilty at my sense of relief that Mrs. Halprin was finally leaving me alone. I snatched the cup and placed it in her steady hand.

She then smiled with what seemed a false pleasure as she touched me affectionately on the cheek. "I know I can count on you, Paul."

It was far into the early afternoon, after I had dug a few more graves and sensed a new calm had settled over the cemetery. I returned to the office and spied the well-worn sign that was periodically hung from the drinking water faucet.

Do Not Use—Typhoid!

I tried not to think of Mrs. Halprin, and the final smile she had bestowed on me.

TRUST ME . . . I AM YOUR FRIEND.
WE ARE KINDRED SPIRITS.

The Gathering

I walked my bike over the cobblestoned driveway as I had been doing for many Saturdays since last fall when I agreed to work on the Tombstone Tea project with Miss Mary. She said all of the right things that day, after I slipped back into the office as my mother was saying her good-bye. My mother's eyebrows formed perfect twin arches as she heard my offer to volunteer on the project.

"Despite our new relationship with your high school, we hardly ever get young people in here," Miss Mary had said sadly, peering through her 1950s glasses that were much too large for her tiny face. "But if you can get your classmates involved, we can change all of that," she added, brightening. "I am so glad you see how important the past is, Jessie."

I'm not sure that I was thinking about the past, unless Paul was included in that category. And maybe if I had a project to work on at school, I could make some *real* friends, even if they had to be history buffs.

She raised both of her hands to delicately primp at the halo of white hair about her head, before turning to pick up a sheet of paper. Miss Mary looked old enough to be my great-grandmother, but the way she moved about was fast and light. She was hard to figure out.

"Would you mind writing down your address and phone number?" she asked. "I like to keep a list of our volunteers." Just like that, Miss Mary had recruited me, despite her bizarre request to call her Miss Mary instead of a Miss *something*, as if she were some character out of a southern novel. Yet, despite her weird ways, I liked her.

What was she thinking, I wondered, as I often caught her sliding a glimpse at me and then stealing a look at the photo of Paul on the history board. She'd smile brightly each time, as if pleased that she knew some secret. Her eyes would then disappear into just one more crease in a confluence of crow's-feet.

I parked and locked my bicycle on the rack outside of the office, placing my helmet on top of the seat. It was already hot for early May, and I felt the sweat bead beneath my hair. But I did love the way the cemetery looked in the spring. A soft fuzz of green and white buds settled on the trees like snow, and the harshness of the gray tombstones and other statues that rose from the hills like barren rocks and sticks had faded against the onslaught of new grass and supple blue sky. The air held the smell of soil and flower shop, and the perky chirps of birds obviously thrilled with the arrival of spring.

I was here on that Saturday afternoon to do research, as I had been for many of the past Saturdays. Miss Mary had asked me to gather biographical information on a number of famous Philadelphians buried here. She thought that my classmates and I could perform quick reenactments of some of the more interesting people as a part of the new Tombstone Tea. The whole idea was similar to what Paul had claimed the real spirits were doing on that night last fall. *Had the spirits been performing their own Tombstone Tea?*

I was tasked with writing the scripts, and incredibly, I had talked Michelle, Jeanne, and Melanie into performing some of the roles. They had been shocked when I presented them with the complete set of rubbing's after my night in the cemetery—of course, I didn't share the true story. They acquired a new respect for me, for in their eyes I was either insanely brave or crazy or both, which made me worth knowing. And the three of them needed the bonus points in history to get the As they were striving for to maintain their GPAs. They were even helping me to recruit additional actors.

Strangely enough, I felt content at the cemetery despite that nighttime adventure last fall. Somehow, and I have to believe that it's thanks to Paul, I was left with the more lasting impression that the cemetery celebrates life through its insistence on remembering the once living. The scary stuff had somehow receded.

When I thought about Adam Forepaugh and Elisha Kane, and all the others that showed themselves when Paul was rushing me to the gate, I think they needed me. Or needed another living person like me to recognize their existence and their place in the world. Only Jenny had left me feeling threatened, as her spirit smothered like a cold, obliterating shadow.

Because of Jenny, I still wouldn't come to the cemetery at night. And when I thought about that night here when Paul was at my side, even when the sun shone through the curtains of my bedroom window as I sat on my bed working on the scripts, the fact that I saw dead people could stop me cold. I've never told my parents about that and I hadn't seen any spirits since. I wasn't really sure that I wanted to see them again—except for Paul.

I had suggested researching Elisha Kent Kane and Adam Forepaugh to Miss Mary and she nodded almost knowingly. I would go by their mausoleums regularly, which seemed weird since I felt like I knew them. And to have actually seen them was even weirder. I never went near Jenny's grave, which was beside her daughter's and that little black angel statue with the curly hair and cherub smile. That was the spot where I first saw Paul, but because of Jenny, I avoided it now like dark closets and bug-filled basements.

"Pull out the tidbits of their lives that would make you think that they were *cool*, Jessie. We're trying to get more kids like you and your friends to visit," Miss Mary had suggested. "We need young people to understand that the dead were just like us." When Miss Mary said "cool," she made me feel as if we were part of a Buddy Holly movie or something. Maybe it was her 1950s glasses that made me think of the singer who sang "That'll Be The Day" and died in that plane crash just when he was becoming really famous. If Buddy Holly had been buried here, I'd make sure he was a part of the Tombstone Tea.

And even though I was still skeptical, since I am not such a history fan myself, I was surprised to find out that

I liked this work. I was amazed to learn about Elisha's and Adam's accomplishments, acts of bravery, and the tragedy in their lives. I guess it's because they weren't just dead people in a history book that were buried here. They were dead people that I had met. I could touch the walls of their resting place. It kind of made me realize that the dead were real people with passions and problems—just like me.

I tried researching Paul, but found only two records about him or his parents. His family disappeared after Paul's death. They had sold their house by Eastern State Penitentiary—the first large prison of its kind, built in 1829. A medieval fortress-like structure from the outside, from the air it looked like a stone wagon wheel, its spokes designed to be individual prison cells. My mother told me that the Quakers, who developed this prison system, thought that solitary confinement was necessary for prisoners to reflect on and repent their sins. Thus the word *penitentiary,* she liked to smugly point out, as the prisoners were considered penitents. The prison still stands today. The house deed was one document I was able to find. And the other was an obituary for Paul that I dug out right here in the cemetery's archives. Unfortunately, all it said was that he worked at the cemetery and died at sixteen from typhoid. There was no information on where he was buried. Miss Mary is sure that he's buried somewhere here in the cemetery, but no one has ever found a grave or marker. I didn't dare show Miss Mary the rubbing from Paul's tombstone he had placed in my backpack last fall. I had searched for his grave every Saturday, to no avail.

Miss Mary had since given me a few more names to research. I liked to start my work by walking through the cemetery to find their graves and marking my notebook with little observations I made. For some reason, I preferred to know where they were resting before I learned their histories. I also knew that, as always, she would have a cool glass of lemonade waiting for me when I got back to the office.

I began to walk the steep path that formed the spine of the cemetery ridge turning south, along the driveway that ran past Elisha's mausoleum toward "Millionaire's Row." Already, my jeans and T-shirt were damp and the wisps of hair that touched my neck were annoying. I had only just reached the highest point of the hill, not far from Adam's mausoleum, when I heard him.

"You need to be careful."

I spun around to see Paul, looking as cool as a ghost,

standing by the curb in the denim pants and a flannel shirt similar to the one that he wore last fall. His complexion was a pale gray—the color of death—making his dark hair and cool blue eyes all the more pronounced. Why had I not noticed that before? He smiled at me as if he were glad to see me, then suddenly became serious.

I stumbled, feeling weak in the knees. I had wanted to see Paul again so badly, since that day when I saw his photograph on the office wall. I had waited months to talk to him and had so many questions that I replayed in my head every weekend when I walked these grounds. Why had he appeared to me now? What had happened that night between him and the other spirits after he had pushed me through the gate? Questions that I knew would tumble from my lips one after another. But seeing him now, knowing that he truly was a spirit, scared me all over again.

My knees buckled and I fell butt down on the lawn.

"Are you all right?" he asked, rushing toward me. He extended his hands as if to grasp my own and pull me up. I gasped, as his arms still bore the fine scratches. They frightened me, as they looked like the marks left by a cornered wild animal.

"You scared me" was all I could say.

By his smile, he looked glad to see me. It wasn't a smile of someone laughing at you for doing something stupid. It was the smile of a good friend that you haven't seen in a while. My heart seemed to do a little jump. My blood pulsed as if pleased by his smell—that pungent aroma of evergreens.

"Sorry. I forget you're new at this. I'll try to be more careful until you get used to it all," he said. Now his smile took on a sheepish quality as he pulled me to my feet.

"Used to what?" I asked, fearful of the answer, as I bent to pick up my notebook and brushed it off.

"Used to your . . . gift. You're like me, you know, although not as strong yet, but I can't imagine that taking very long." His blue eyes were suddenly incredibly sincere.

"What are you talking about?" I asked, my voice rising, as I almost knew the answer.

"That you are a spiritualist. You can communicate with the dead, of course. You can sense their spirits—sometimes see them, just as I did." He was somber again, an adult talking to a scared child. I got the feeling that he was leaning toward me, even though he wasn't that much taller. "Why do you think you can see me or see Elisha and Adam as you did, if you do not have the gift?"

I thought about the feelings and images that would

flood my mind at my old school—those sensations that made me appear to be a daydreamer zoning out in the middle of class. *But a spiritualist?* I didn't want to be one of those strange people who spent their time huddled around a table in a séance summoning the dead. From what I had read, there were plenty of them running around about a hundred years ago. But most people had made fun of them because they were either fakes or crazy.

I must have turned white, for Paul grabbed my hands as if I might fall again.

"I'm a spiritualist, Jessie. It's a good thing if you truly have the gift. You have the chance to bring peace to the living and the dead."

"I don't want that, Paul. I don't want to see dead people. I only want to see you." And if I had truly lost my color, now I could feel it all rushing back to my face. Paul was a dead person, and here I was spending my free time hanging around a cemetery in the hopes that he—who was the only person my age that I felt a real connection to—would show his face. And now that he had, I wanted to hug him *and* run from him.

But instead I stalled. "And I haven't see them, spirits I mean, since last fall . . . except for you right now," I added weakly.

"Because you don't want to. I understand. It's unsettling to say the least." He smiled once more and looked so pleased that I could see him do so.

"Where have you been?" I asked, surprised at the sudden hurt in my voice. Again a part of me wanted to disappear from embarrassment. I was aching as if he were my stupid boyfriend.

"Why, watching you . . . and watching Jenny, of course. I needed to find out what she intends to do."

"You know how to ruin a moment, Paul," I blurted, still acting out the wounded girlfriend part. It was only because of Jenny that he decided to make an appearance.

"Jessie." Now he reached out to grab my arm, just as he did that night last fall when he tried to convince me to stay with him in the cemetery to get the rubbings. "You know how dangerous she is." His eyes beseeched that I believe him. "I know that you still must sense her . . . interest in you."

I pulled my arm away from him. A breeze, the first that I felt that day, played with the few still dry strands of my hair. I thought I heard the soft laughter of a woman in my ear, which made me forget all about my schizo feelings for Paul.

"Stop it!" I shouted, at Paul, at the teasing breeze.

"Jenny's daughter died at sea, and no matter how hard she tries, she can't change that history!" Jenny had taken me to that ship—had tried to force me into the lifeboat that her own daughter refused. I knew he couldn't argue with that. He more than anyone knew that truth.

"She may have died at sea, Jessie," he said gently, careful not to reach for me again. "But Jenny doesn't share everything about Amy's death. The truth was too much for her to bear," he whispered.

For a moment, all I could hear was a fearsome howl in my ears. The grass and trees surrounding us stood petrified. I could see that Paul was still speaking but no words reached my ear.

He must have seen the look of horror on my face because he turned and shouted angrily at something or someone, past the cobblestoned lane of house-sized mausoleums, where the roadway dips back toward the Entrance House and Jenny's and Amy's graves.

The wind stopped and I could hear the birds again, oblivious to all forces except nature's spring. But I knew all too well that Jenny was anything but natural.

"Take my hand, Jessie. Trust me as you did that night. I am your friend. We are kindred spirits." And at this he smiled, pleased to find me by his side.

"We are meant to do this together. I knew this as soon as I found you crouching against that black little angel that was the start of all these troubles."

I had longed to hear these words from Paul every Saturday that I had passed through the cemetery gate. But suddenly I was spooked at the thought of being a spiritualist like Paul—someone that the dead would be attracted to.

"What is it?" he asked of my silence, reaching for my hand to hold it. His touch was smooth and cool.

"It's daytime, Paul. These weird sorts of things are only supposed to happen at night."

His smile was sympathetic yet knowing. "She's tired of waiting, Jessie. As was I. But now you and I are going to fix things here."

Normally, when people use phrases like "fix things," I assume they mean buying stuff at Home Depot, or worse, sitting down for a heart-to-heart. "Fixing things" was hardly the phrase I would have chosen to connote banishing a crazed and malevolent spirit from the living and spiritual world. But Paul had given me my assignment and the following Saturday had been the due date.

Miss. Mary looked at me expectantly when I came through the office door. She had been busy arranging coffee mugs and T-shirts with the Laurel Hill Cemetery logo on the office counter for the next tour of the resting sites and incredible statuary of Philadelphia's famous and infamous. Oddly enough, the logo was a cherubic angel's face alighted on wings. I glanced in the direction of Amy's and Jenny's graves.

"How are you doing today, dear?" She dipped her head meaningfully, her eyes magnified behind her winged glasses. She was wearing a white short-sleeved blouse sprinkled with flower patterns. A fan was propped on the opposite counter, causing her short, white, thin, teased hair to tremble about her face. But despite her appearance of fragility, I sensed a steeliness about her that I had never picked up before.

It was another brilliant, sunny day, hot as the previous Saturday. We both looked out into the small parking area to see the knot of people from the earlier tour fanning themselves with their brochures. They were mostly older people, older than my own parents, but they were smiling and talking. They looked flushed and animated from the exertion and the new appreciation that such tours bring to the cemetery.

Instead of answering Miss Mary's question, it was easier for me to remark on this distraction. "They look as if they enjoyed themselves, Miss Mary." I stared out the window to ensure she got my meaning.

She only sighed.

"There are no youngsters among them, Jessie. You'll soon help us change that."

She smiled at me in her normal sweet way, the smile that promised a lemonade at the end of the day. But her tone was full of the grave.

"I'm doing my best," I said, perhaps a bit too quickly. I felt a little tug of guilt since I had done the research that Paul had asked me to do instead of hers. "I'm going to head out now," I added, grabbing my notebook.

"Of course, dear," she replied, stealing a look at that photo of Paul just before I had turned to push open the office screen door.

Paul had told me to research old newspaper and society page articles about Jenny Halprin. I had found plenty of photographs and announcements about her, some the Central Library archivist had told me were scandalous for the times. Jenny and Mr. Halprin at society balls. Jenny going solo to a variety of fund-raisers for orphans and hospitals. There was even a photograph of Jenny with presidential nominee Theodore Roosevelt—a Roosevelt for President banner strung over her and a dozen other women's heads. The photos, of course, were black and white. Jenny was always dressed in beautiful gowns, her blond hair elegantly done above her head. She forever held a glass of champagne or wine. I never found her obituary. The documentation of her life stopped after Amy's death.

I stared hard at these photos to make sure that my eyes weren't blurring. In many of them I noticed a shadow a few steps behind her, no matter her pose or how many other people were crammed into the photograph. I asked the archivist about this but he couldn't see it.

"It was death," Paul told me. We were sitting in our now favorite spot in the cemetery—the section of lawn that thrust itself over Kelly Drive, named in 1985 after the actress Grace Kelly's brother, John B. Kelly Junior, an Olympic rower and city councilman. A fence, of course, kept us and visitors from tumbling over the cliffed walls. The Schuylkill River flowed in front of us today, serene and filled with oarsmen in their long, fragile boats. Their sculls seemed to barely touch the water. Behind us was a row of mausoleums, including Elisha's.

I shivered, despite the sun-baked shade. The birds

were singing and chattering all around us as May had lost all memory of the cold. I was wearing a tank top and jeans. What clothes was a person supposed to wear when speaking of death?

"How do you know that?" I asked. I wished I had the copies of the newspaper articles with me then for Paul to point out the things I couldn't see.

"Because she took her life as her daughter did. Jenny knew she was going to do that all along," he said matter-of-factly.

I stared at his smooth-as-a-statue skin. He was looking out toward the river his chin thrust forward and his hair just pushed back from his forehead.

Sometimes he looked so much older. "You asked me to find some clues, some weakness of Jenny's," I reminded him. "She didn't seem to have time for weakness."

Now he turned to look at me. "Only that she was hurtling herself towards death," Paul said, as if agreeing with me. "There was no precaution or hesitancy in her life, and she seemed to care for nothing." He trailed off, as if unsure of this last thought.

"Except for her daughter," I said before Paul could.

"We may need Amy," Paul replied.

If I was chilled before, I was now cold inside. I pulled

my knees beneath my chin and gave him a sideways glance.

"What do you mean, Paul? Are you talking about *summoning* Amy?"

He reached out and touched my chin, gently guiding it so that I was looking at him straight on.

"I spoke with Elisha last night. He agrees. If you and I were unable to discover something new about Jenny, something that she cared about in life that we could entice her spirit to grab, then we would have to find another way to provide Jenny with peace." He stared into my eyes. His brows were furrowed. "All the causes she seemed to support and the parties and galas that she attended were diversions. If Jenny were looking for something to make herself whole again, she obviously didn't find it." Paul sighed, as if he knew this all along. "Jenny has craved her daughter's forgiveness since Amy's death. If we wish to bring peace back to this cemetery, and protect the living who visit it, Amy will need to forgive her mother. It's all we have to work on."

"That's crazy," I said, pushing his hand from my knee. He held it to ensure my attention. His touch was incredibly light.

Paul had told me what Jenny had done to her daughter. I had thought of Mom, about how I would have felt if my own mother had done such a thing to me. The idea made me sick to my stomach. "She will never forgive her mother," I said with certainty.

Paul shook his head. "I said the same thing to Elisha, but he wasn't so sure. You see, Elisha had connected with Amy somehow, that night one hundred years ago when we asked her to help rid the cemetery of her mother." Paul sighed with what seemed regret. "Elisha knew that Amy had refused to speak with her mother through me. She told him that she would never allow her living mother such a privilege. Not even upon her mother's death. . . ."

He turned away from me to gaze at the Schuylkill again. I detected a wistfulness in his voice. "Amy never planned to allow me to help her move on. If Jenny had known that, I doubt she would have given me that glass of typhoid water or have quenched her own thirst with it."

This time I touched his knee. "I'm sorry, Paul. How truly awful for you," I said, a shiver in my voice. I realized that he was the victim of a family quarrel that reached beyond the living. Yet it was the living that were lethal to one another.

He turned back to me and smiled. His blue eyes were gentle as he said, "But I was given a new cause, and Elisha tells me that Amy needed more time. He thinks she's ready for us to reach out for her help."

I stood up. This talk of ringing up the dead Amy was giving me the creeps.

———— ·◆· ————

"How are we going to do this, Paul? Are we going to run down to her grave, right next to her mother's and the little black angel statue, and have a séance?" I desperately looked out to the Schuylkill, to its rowers blissfully tugging at the river like water striders. The normal world was right in front of my face, but it didn't appear that my place was in that world. Maybe I wasn't really a spiritualist but just a girl who gets distracted easily. Maybe I was allowing Paul to drag me into his world because when I was with him I felt good.

I spun back around to look at Paul, who was still sitting cross-legged on the grass. On the earthen terrace above him was the row of mausoleums and a line of tombstones, standing in formation. He offered me a sympathetic smile, his blue eyes suddenly sparkling with mischief.

"Of course we're not going to have a séance, Jessie. We'll have a meeting early tonight, right here by Elisha's place."

I hadn't been in a joking mood but it turned out that Paul had been completely serious. This is how they "called back" the resting dead in an emergency, he explained. The active spirits of the cemetery would get together after dusk and collectively focus on the spirit they were seeking. "It's kind of like sending a message to the other side," he said. "If I did it alone, my signal would be weak, but if we get a committee together, particularly a committee of the cemetery's most active spirits, we'll resound like an orchestra."

I was looking at Paul as if he were out of his mind. "What if someone else picks up the message, someone like Jenny?" I asked. The whole thing sounded ridiculous.

"Well, there is that risk," he admitted. "But we will be careful and we'll have your added voice to help us."

I didn't know what to say, but I could feel my legs trembling, despite the long-sleeved shirt I had pulled over my tank top. After Paul told me about the meeting, I had gone back to the office, picked up my bike, and said good night to Miss Mary, who gave me an odd wink with her good-bye wave. I went home for a quick dinner and told my parents that I had to return tonight to help out with a "twilight tour." My mom made sure I took my cell phone so that I could call her when I was ready to be picked up.

She would throw the bike on the car rack.

But now I was standing with Paul by Elisha's mausoleum, my favorite place not looking all that safe and peaceful anymore. I hadn't been in the cemetery at night since last fall, and I had forgotten how the early evening shadows seemed to make the white tombstones and obelisks glow as if they had been solar powered. Even the delicate white buds of the trees stood out against the purple sky. The Schuylkill River was becoming harder to see, as headlights from the cars flew up and down Kelly Drive, muting all else with their glare.

"Paul, I am scared," I pronounced. "I don't know if I can do this."

He was shoulder to shoulder with me in a second.

"I will not leave your side," he promised. "You are a lot stronger and braver than you give yourself credit for. The gathering will begin in just a few moments."

I nodded and held my breath, peering into the lustrous shadows of the stones watching for movement. Any kind of movement.

Paul was right. All too soon I saw the shimmering wisps of what initially looked like vapor, rising from the earth from multiple graves or escaping barred mausoleum windows and doors. The gleaming steam-like substance kept close to the ground and began to float toward us from every direction. It reminded me of the summer mist that moves on the surface of a lake just before it is burned off by the sun's heat. But at a lake, there are cabins filled with people and families vacationing together. Except for the caws of those big black crows that hung out in the cemetery, I felt like I was the only living being in the world.

Paul touched my elbow. "Let's move over there," he whispered as he pointed to the spot in front of us where the grass grew thick with a deeper green than the rest of the lawn that sloped toward the bowl. Knee-high tombstones ringed the circular depression suggesting a campfire setting. Just beyond the concave depression was the high cyclone fencing and Kelly Drive below.

"And Jessie," he added quickly, "don't watch the spirits gather, as this is your first time. It might seem a bit unnerving."

I nodded, but couldn't keep from glancing over my shoulder to see a now fully flowing stream of radiant white vapor cascading down the steps of the terrace. The stream was incandescent and cast a soft light on the ground and the tombstones it flowed past. I must have gasped, for Paul chided, "Jessie."

I should have been babbling hysterically as Paul gently guided me to sit on the smooth sill of one of the campfire tombstones, my back to the Schuylkill River, but I wasn't afraid as I had expected. Despite having a now unobstructed view of stray strands of vapor that spun purposely into the ghostly forms of the once living, I was relatively calm. Paul took his place on the tombstone beside me and he reached out to take my hand. One by one, the tombstones edging the border of the circle became occupied.

This was the moment I had dreaded since last fall. I sat mesmerized by the wraithlike procession. The cemetery behind the scene looked oddly transformed. The outlines of the mausoleums, obelisks, gravestones, and more strikingly the trees that thrust their branches into the night sky appeared electrified like a black-and-white negative lit from behind. The air smelled of a thousand matches struck simultaneously. A crow cawed accusingly. *Jenny*? I wondered.

"Are you okay?" Paul whispered to me. I couldn't answer. I didn't know what I was feeling. I was trembling from head to toe and my heart was beating fast enough to take my breath away. Yet I didn't want to run. I wanted to stay to see and hear from the spirits that had troubled my thoughts since last fall. Only then I realized that I had not been preoccupied so much from the fear of them as from the knowledge that they existed and had shown themselves to me.

The streaming had stopped and now I willed myself to turn from Paul to look at the figure who was sitting on the tombstone beside me.

"Hello, dear," she nodded with a smile. She was less solid than Paul, so much so that I could just barely make out the faint outline of the branches of a fir tree through her back. Unlike Paul, she was more like a film image projected against the night, although she was close enough that I could see that her graying hair sported those fussy pressed curls of the actresses in the old movies. She was wearing a matronly dress with a pearl necklace and sensible shoes. Her eyes were incredibly kind. "It's good to see you here. My name is Marian." She then looked at me expectantly.

I'm not sure if I smiled back but I think I returned the nod.

There were six of us seated about the bowl, including Paul and me. The other four were women, equally transparent, of various ages, the youngest a bit older than me. I could pass her on the street without a second glance. She had long dark hair, parted in the middle, and was wearing a crinoline hippie skirt and a blouse with puffy sleeves. She could have walked right out of the 1970s but it was a look that was back in fashion. The other two were in "period costumes," as my mother would say if we were visiting a place like Colonial Williamsburg. But as my history is not as fine-tuned as my mom's, I could only make broad guesses. I'd have to say the nineteenth century— long dresses, hair pulled back in chignons with a waterfall of curls cascading against their cheeks. They perched themselves on the edge of their tombstone chairs with their backs straight and their heads held high, as if they were at someone's table for dinner. Marian and the young woman looked to have shared a century.

Suddenly I was startled by a sparrow flying right through one of the women's heads. I tried not to think about their lack of physical substance.

Paul suddenly stood. "Forgive us, ladies. I regret that I need to make expedient introductions, as Elisha and Adam are due to begin our meeting at any moment. We'll have ample time in the future to make acquaintances."

I felt my eyebrows prick in surprise at Paul's fancy language. And then I noticed that the women had all turned to look at me pointedly. Only Marian smiled. All I could think about then was how important it was for me to stay calm if I were truly a spiritualist as Paul had insisted. A spiritualist was supposed to *enjoy* speaking to the dead.

As he spoke, a warm breeze kicked up. I watched as it played with the women's hair and tugged at their dresses. The air suddenly smelled of fertile earth and trees as it does before a summer storm. Lightning flashed in the sky. One of the women was humming, at least I guessed it to be one of the women, in a low, flat tune like a monk's chant. My skin turned to gooseflesh.

Paul interrupted the spell. "You have already met Marian."

"Indeed she did," Marian quickly agreed. "I know Jessie will be helpful, as you have been, Paul." Another flash of the heat lightning touched the sky. There was no thunder, but the momentary flare revealed Marian's translucent skin so that I could see the trace of blue veins in her temples. She reached out to touch my hand and I flinched involuntarily. I was even more unnerved when I felt nothing.

I looked to catch Paul's attention. What did this mean? But he was already addressing the nineteenth-century women. Each looked to be around my mother's age, in their early forties, I guessed. Both had long red hair. They wore no makeup, yet they had a natural, soft beauty. Their resemblance was striking, even to the haunted look in their eyes. The next flash of lightning revealed a splattering of red on their bodices and skirts. Surely not blood, I thought. These women were spirits, not actors in some horror flick, but my heart continued to pound anyway.

"Eleanor and Claire are sisters, Jessie. Both served as nurses to the wounded soldiers at the Civil War Battle of Gettysburg. They each lost a betrothed in that battle," Paul noted softly. "The horror of the deaths they witnessed were pressed onto their souls."

Eleanor and Claire, I didn't know which one was which, nodded at me gravely. I saw they held each other's hands.

"I'm sorry," was all I could whisper. I'm not even sure if I said it aloud.

"And this is Cindy," Paul began more brightly.

"Hey, Jessie," she interrupted, before Paul could finish. "I was killed by a drunk driver when I was in college and I'm still really pissed about it. I've got to do something with my anger."

I didn't know what to say to that. This could have been one of those support group meetings you saw in the movies, except this little group covered all sorts of bases. I looked back to Marian, as I still didn't know her story. None of these women were on my research list for Miss Mary.

"Murder," she informed me helpfully. "My husband. He really deserved it," she added, straightening her skirt. "It was well worth the death penalty I received."

Paul cleared his throat. "Now that we've all had a chance to meet. . . ."

The wind strengthened, cutting Paul short. Dust and blades of grass swirled about us as if the six of us were in the eye of a small tornado.

And the chanting had ceased, replaced now by the low, howling wind. The mixture of soil particles and slices of grass and leaves created a dust storm around us. I could no longer see the cemetery beyond, and the periodic flashes of lightning were reduced to a gray, strobe-like shadow.

The spirits in our circle looked unfazed. Only Paul's eyes gleamed expectantly.

Suddenly Elisha and Adam stepped through the wind-fueled curtain as simply as if walking through an open door. They appeared as solidly as I had remembered them—Elisha, a frosty, full beard impinging on wind-burned cheeks, dressed in a bulky coat that looked like today's parkas and with mittens the size of baseball gloves, and Adam, thick and scruffy, a rounder version of Abraham Lincoln with a tic. I found that I was glad to see them, especially Elisha. I had done so much research on them—Elisha Kent Kane, the Arctic adventurer, and Adam Forepaugh, the circus master. Even though it sounded crazy, I felt I knew them both.

"Forgive us for the theatrics, Jessie. Jenny knows that we are plotting, and we must do our best to keep her in the dark."

They all left in the same way they came, by way of an ectoplasm rivulet. Elisha ended the meeting, and with this adjournment, the spirits suddenly dissolved to slump and sliver from their respective tombstones to run to the glowing, vaporous stream that flowed back to the main cemetery grounds.

With the spirits' departure, a stunned silence seemed to inhabit the cemetery. Paul, Elisha, Adam, and I were sitting cross-legged by Elisha's mausoleum, as I had refused to sit on the slimed grass by the campfire tombstones. All around us, the cemetery was lit by the mausoleums that glowed from their windows and doors like Chinese lanterns. It was as if someone had decided to flick a switch and put on the party lights only after the party was over.

I was breathless, even without expending any effort toward speech. But my heart was panting as if I had sprinted two miles. I was telling myself that for a spiritualist this was normal but I couldn't convince my body that I wasn't freaked out. What did people say about instinct? To trust it, right?

The silence pricked at my back, and I needed to break it. Questions were piling up in my mind about the spirits I had just met and this bizarre *committee meeting* that I was sitting through. Maybe some answers would help quell some of my fears. I turned to Paul.

"Why are the women so . . . shimmery?" I asked. "Why are they not . . . as real looking as you and Elisha and Adam?"

"They're not as strongly bound to this world as we are. It's by choice, Jessie. They are already flickering between the two worlds, a sign that they are ready to move on." Paul seemed pleased at my question. He smiled encouragingly at me, like one of my goofy teachers.

"But all the lingering spirits still lend their support," Elisha interrupted. "They know that we are planning now. They're giving us their spiritual guidance as well as providing a distraction." Elisha pointed to the glow in the dark mausoleums.

"Okay," I nodded, struggling to ignore the chattering of my teeth. So far, having more information wasn't calming my nerves. "Why were only women spirits invited to this meeting?" I felt ridiculous using that word for what seemed to be the equivalent of a séance in the cemetery.

"Ahhh, Jessie, because this is a woman's riddle, of course," Elisha retorted. "There are plenty of men in this cemetery who would materialize in a minute to answer this committee's summons. They are all around us." Elisha made a sweeping motion with his arm. "They are the inhabitants of the vast majority of the mausoleums and crypts that occupy this place."

"And so they glow to send you a message to remind you that they are here?" I asked, perhaps a bit too skeptically.

And then, just for a moment, I sensed them all, too—the spirits waiting in the wings for their invitation to join us. I felt their unseen fingers touch my hair, caress my face, tug at my clothes. Heated, anxious whispers filled my ears, while the smell of earth and evergreen trees, a thousand times stronger than Paul's friendly scent, filled my nostrils.

I leaped up, swatting at the air to push them back. I must have screamed, because Paul grabbed my arm and pulled me down.

"It's okay, Jessie. The spirits touch all living things, but because you are a spiritualist, you can feel them. You'll learn how to shake them off like an annoying cobweb in time. But they mean you no harm," he assured me.

"If you could wipe that look of horror off your face, which Adam and I feel quite insulted by, I will continue," Elisha sniffed. Adam, eyes blinking, nodded in agreement.

"Don't be so tough, Elisha," Paul scolded, wrapping his arm around my shoulder. "This *is* her first night!"

I shivered in Paul's embrace, happy to let him argue my case.

"You weren't quite so jittery," Adam pointed out to Paul with a mischievous smirk.

"My parents were spiritualists, Adam. You know that. They *invited* spirits into our home." Paul stared at Adam, waiting for his response but Adam was already looking up at the silent, dark trees.

"Let's finish this up, Elisha," Paul said sternly.

Elisha barely smiled. But the glint in his eyes was unmistakable.

"Just toughening you up, dear," Elisha said. "Just as we did last fall, although Jenny's abduction of you was not a part of the planned training."

I nodded, still unsure about how to take all this. When Elisha and Adam and all the other spirits were begging me to stay with them—that was training? Not the word I would have used for it at that time.

"Okay, but doesn't Jenny know about the cemetery committee meetings, too?" I shot back, a fresh fear wrapping itself about my spine.

"Only in a very intuitive way," Elisha replied. "She has never been a part of the community here and therefore she only knows its rules from what she can discern as an outsider."

I shivered again, still under Paul's protective arm, but noticed that Adam was looking at me in that hungry way that he did last fall. Maybe I wasn't so glad to see Adam, I thought. He shouldn't behave like those less disciplined spirits, unless he imagined his behavior as more *training*. He must have noticed me slowly shimmying away from him.

"Forgive me, dear. I can't help but be attracted to your life force. Some of us 'pulsing blood' addicts are not as well disciplined as Paul and Elisha." He licked his lips, and his tiny little eyes blinked as if someone had suddenly trained a bright light on his face. "I'm still a bit more of a 'common' spirit." I grabbed Paul's hand.

Paul glanced at me and gave me a look that said, "I'll explain later." *Pulsing blood addicts?* I didn't like the sound of that. Was I a substance that the spirits wanted to devour when I least expected it? No, I reminded myself. Paul told me that I was a spiritualist. I was important to the spirits, as I was able to represent them in the living world. So maybe they were just a little bit out of practice with normal human behavior. For some of them, it had been more than one hundred years. I was hanging my future on that hopeful thought. I looked back to Paul for reassurance, but he had already looked away and was gazing at Elisha expectantly.

"It is time to review the recommendations of the committee," Elisha announced, suddenly grave. He rubbed his nose as if to make sure that the poor frozen thing was still there.

"Let's begin with Marian's advice," he offered. "To sum up, Marian, not surprisingly, recommended that we crush Jenny's spirit. She believed that the daughter will join us in devising her mother's demise."

"Yes," Adam sneered. "She said that Jenny, like her

dearly departed husband, was treacherous. That Marian was 'my kind of woman,'" Adam laughed.

Elisha raised a frosted eyebrow as he continued. "Claire and Eleanor, as they are nurses who witnessed the carnage wrought by war among brothers, and are good souls inherently, advised us to work a reconciliation between Jenny and her daughter. Time is infinite, they noted, and any transgression can be sutured and healed."

I did my best to keep my thoughts away from the sisters' bloodied bodices. They had looked as if they had been splashed in the blood of an entire nation's wounds. How durable could a misunderstanding between a mother and daughter really be, they had asked?

Paul summed up Cindy's advice. "She just insisted that we needed to set Amy straight. Her logic is what's one stolen boyfriend in the grand scheme of things? Cindy couldn't believe that Amy had killed herself over that," Paul said, shaking his head.

"She did say that Jenny's daughter needed to get real," I added, which was kind of jarring to hear a spirit speak in a modern way. People shouldn't die over such drama, Cindy had insisted. *Poor Cindy*, I thought. Her life had been cut short by a stranger's own deadly drama.

And then the cemetery's silence embraced us. Paul

and Elisha closed their eyes, as if mulling things over. Adam stared off into the darkness. I strained to hear the faintest breeze or the sound of a car in the distance. I held my breath. Nothing.

But then Elisha broke his trance. His gaze settled on me.

"So, Jessie, based upon the advice of our committee, what would you recommend?" Elisha asked. Adam and Paul said nothing, calmly watching me trying to filter my unsaid thoughts.

Was this a test of my ability as a spiritualist? But then Paul smiled at me, raising his strong chin, telling me to go for it. Adam shot me a hungry grin.

"Everyone's advice is so different," I answered defensively. I racked my brain. My parents had always told me to do the right thing and that the right thing wouldn't cause upset stomachs or guilt. Essentially, it was an "aim to hurt no one" philosophy. That advice seemed good for everyone from living kids to long-dead spirits.

Marian's advice had scared me. Even if it were the right thing to do, how did one go about extinguishing a spirit?

And Cindy's suggestion was impractical. Obviously, Jenny's daughter was not in the mood for forgiveness.

"I think I'm leaning toward the sisters' advice," I said, after clearing my voice. "I think we should see if we can bring Amy and Jenny together again, just to start a conversation. They could use some good counseling," I concluded. I then reddened with embarrassment.

Elisha rubbed his mittens together, a mischievous anticipation glowing in his eyes. "Even if it means a little spilling of some blood?" he asked cryptically.

"What blood?" I asked. We were talking about spirits. And then I noticed he was looking right at me, the only member of the committee who still had some blood to spill.

I CAN'T SEEM TO TOUCH HER . . .

The Summoning

If we hadn't been in a cemetery, I might have thought we were passing through a well-lit ghost town, with the mausoleums and crypts shivering light as we wove our way through them. Were their spirits animated by our quest to reunite Jenny and Amy or were they fearful? It was as if each mausoleum wished to cast its own brightness against the dark.

The cemetery had been silent before when we had gathered for our committee meeting, but it was now bursting with sound—the squawks of birds of prey, the squeals of the hunted, and a cacophony of voices—conversations, laughter, crying, and appeals that had nothing to do with us.

My knees were weak and my heart was in overdrive. Paul once again grabbed my hand as we made our way to Jenny's and Amy's graves.

Waiting for us there were the shimmering women I had met earlier that evening. Each held a tall, slender candle by its elaborate base. They reminded me of the fancy candelabra that graced Victorian millionaires' dinner tables. I fleetingly wondered if the women had raided a few mausoleums. Despite the cool, consistent breeze that now engulfed us, the flames of each candle burned high and unwavering.

I looked at the black angel that seemed to gaze at the women unperturbed. Someone had placed a small candle in the angel's outstretched hand. And there were more candelabras around each grave, as if someone were thinking of dining on the top of the twin grassy mounds.

Paul, Elisha, Adam, and I stood by the dark trunk of the towering sycamore. Elisha and Adam nodded with approval at the Halloween scene before us.

"Jenny was used to elegance and luxury," Eleanor or Claire explained matter-of-factly. "We thought a formal summoning might calm her down."

But Marian seemed impatient. She fussed with her hair a little, patting down her ghostly curls with her hand. "Well, what did you all decide? Will we crush her?" she asked hopefully.

Cindy shifted the candelabra to her other hand and rolled her eyes. She would have looked more natural with a peace sign in her hand.

By now, I was ready to collapse. My legs were like pudding. My beating heart had sapped all my energy. I felt light-headed and wobbly.

"Paul," I whined.

"I'm right here, Jessie. You can do it. We will not leave you."

"You are the only one who can do this, child." Elisha's voice was kind yet commanding. "Only the living can bring these two spirits together."

I emitted a jagged sigh and then bit my lip. You are a spiritualist, I reminded myself, *willing* myself to believe Paul and Elisha. That I indeed had the power to make things right for Jenny and Amy.

"It's time we joined hands," Adam reminded us. He licked his lips, a mannerism that I now recognized as a sign of his gleeful anticipation. He was rough and greedy as he grabbed my free hand. Paul held my other. Elisha extended a hand to the spirits.

"We all must call to Amy together," Elisha instructed, I gathered for my benefit. "Your call is the most alluring, child, as the restless dead have trouble ignoring the call of the living."

We all began chanting her name. I struggled to make my voice more than a whisper.

"Put some oomph into it, dearie," Adam ordered deri-sively.

I did my best to focus, trying to picture the spirit Amy but instead conjuring up the image of the black angel coming to life. The very thought left me horrified, and then was banished. I felt the earth beneath my feet begin to tremble with what I sensed without understanding to be Amy's anger and uncertainty at our communal imposi-tion. I panicked silently, sensing the ebb and flow of Amy's reluctant spirit answering our call—my call in particular. It was a coldness, a sense of foreboding that covered and receded from my body like an electric tide.

The cemetery was disturbed, its only other living creatures—fireflies, ladybugs, moths—suddenly fluttered about the candles in droves or crawled all over the twin white tombstones. Worms and ants squirmed from beneath the soft earth at our feet. Even the birds—nightingales, robins, pigeons, and some bats—perched and hopped from tree to tree, weighing the branches over our heads with their collective morbid curiosity.

There was a moon—not a whole one—but a moon enough to cast a chalky light over the scene about us.

The strong smell of evergreens, sulfur, and rain-soaked earth saturated the air.

I knew Amy was with us when I felt cold hands grasping at my ankles, then the pressure of those hands slowly moving up my legs to my waist as if she were using my body to climb from her grave.

"Paul!" I couldn't stop my terrified scream and instantaneously felt his cool presence press against my body.

"Don't be so mean, Amy," he scolded.

Paul was peering at the earth that was boiling about my feet.

And then she was in front of us, not luminous like the other women spirits but as solid as Paul, Elisha, and Adam.

The women spirits in our summoning circle cooed like birds, or maybe it was the birds that were doing the approving cooing. It was hard for me to tell.

Amy looked incensed. She was dressed in what appeared to be a flowing white nightgown. Her long dark hair fell about her shoulders, entwined by white ribbons. She had beautiful dark eyes that flashed with anger against her pale young face. Her lips, which were as white as her face, were quivering. She looked me dead in the eyes.

"Why have you called me?" she demanded, her voice cracking with emotion. She turned to include all of us, even the women spirits, in her contemptuous gaze.

"Will you never learn?" she seemed to spit at Paul.

"Do you want to sacrifice this one, too?"

Paul looked down, as if he were slapped in the face. Then he recovered, returning her stare.

"I'm here to watch over her," he said. "Otherwise, your mother *will* take her, as she did me."

Paul had told me that Jenny had offered him a poisoned glass of water, just as the evil queen had presented her cursed apple to Snow White. But Paul was not saved by a magic kiss. I felt cold to my core. I wanted to cry out then for my own mother.

Amy then turned to Elisha.

"You know better, Elisha. You knew what she was from the moment you saw her."

Elisha nodded sadly, as if moved by Amy's fury.

"Yes I did, dearie. But I didn't have the power to stop her. She was a living being then. I could do nothing. But this girl. . . ." And he looked at me as if I were the source of all hope.

The others didn't seem to notice the sudden strong gusts of wind that buffeted our bodies and battered the trees, shaking their branches like lifeless rag dolls.

"You do know that she is on to you?" Amy asked tiredly, her hair ribbons flapping in the wind and her gown pressed against her body.

Paul squeezed my hand. He seemed to swell from my life force.

"Amy, we need you to banish your mother from here. You must do whatever you need to do to make that happen," he pleaded.

"No!" I interrupted, despite myself. I wanted to be true to the sentiment of the sisters, Eleanor and Claire, who would forever bear the blood of their convictions on their chests. "We need you to forgive your mother. We believe that only then will she be able to move on, once she knows that you will join her."

My heart seemed to stop, anticipating Amy's explosive reaction. But she only wrinkled her nose in disgust, as if looking at us all like a gathering of vermin.

"Surely you know how ridiculous that is. I hate my mother. I will to the end of eternity," she said with a simmering conviction.

If I had been less terrified, I might have been able to predict the results. A bolt of lightning struck the ground just a few yards away from us. A sycamore tree split and toppled near the grave site, falling across the cobblestoned driveway, cutting us off from the Entrance House and cemetery exit. The smell of burning wood and sulfur stung my nostrils. The candles arrayed around the graves and in the black angel's hand flared and then burnt out. For a moment, only the dim light of the moon continued to illuminate our gathering around the graves. I noticed with horror that the black angel's cherubic smile looked disturbedly excited.

The women spirits, who stood behind Amy's back, inhaled like living beings. From the corner of my eye, I could see Elisha and Adam motioning the women to step back, as Elisha and Adam were doing. Paul, however, stayed by my side, whispering to me, "I am not going to leave you."

And then a searing light blazed about the graves like a crashing meteorite, blinding me momentarily with its brilliance and scorching heat. I would have fallen if Paul had not caught me.

"Mother!" I heard Amy scream. "You are vile!"

The spirit women were babbling in excited whispers that seemed magnified by the wind. I heard *Run!* and *Forgive!* above the howling noise. Through the cloud of light that hovered over the graves now, I saw the forms of Elisha and Adam hustling the women to one side, badgering them "to be still."

It was then that I clearly heard Paul say, "Mrs. Halprin!"

And there she stood beside her scowling daughter, as

full-bodied as her Amy. She was wearing the same high-collared white nightgown that she had worn last fall when chasing me through the cemetery. Her white face seemed to reflect the moon, and the purple hollows beneath her eyes added a heartbreaking gauntness that was missing from her society page photographs.

"You know I want nothing to do with you," Amy taunted her. I cringed as Jenny flinched at the words.

"I will change that, dear, as you know I don't feel the same way," she replied with a forced serenity.

And then Jenny turned her gaze on me.

"Be careful of what you do, Mother," Amy warned ominously.

Something tugged at my sleeve and then on the tail of my shirt, although nothing that I could see approached me. Jenny gave me a sly smile.

"Be ready, girl," Elisha growled, and as he raised his bearded chin my way, I felt those unseen hands abandon my clothes to slip through my body to wrap their cold fingers around my heart, my tongue, my veins, and my lungs, spontaneously erupting into thousands of hands grasping greedily at all parts of me. A putrid taste was on my lips and the spirits and tombstones around me began to quiver and fade until the moonlit darkness paled and seared into a burnt orange light. I reached out for Paul's hand but there was no one there.

Something propelled me into the air, yet this air was not the same space that I lived in. This air was devoid of all sound, smell, and temperature. Suddenly I felt suspended in a silent blackness. I blinked but couldn't tell if my eyes were open or closed—until the lights appeared like incandescent stars in a faraway galaxy. At first they grew dim and then bright again, pulsing like a beating heart. Some began to move, dropping and then shooting straight up, or swirling in tiny circles like a moth around candlelight. The lights were hypnotic, as they were all that existed to keep the smothering blackness at bay. I felt surrounded by a universe of fireflies.

Then I was bumped, shoved, and grabbed. I cried out to see Amy shaking her head tiredly at my predicament. "You will not stop, will you? Why does it always have to be about other people's needs?" she growled. I was speechless, as my mind scrambled to remember just what I was supposed to do with her. She floated alongside me now as a full-bodied person—her cheeks red, her eyes a warm brown. She stared at me with an abiding sympathy. "Do you know where you are?" she asked.

I opened my mouth but heard nothing. I shook my

head. I would have guessed that I was dead, but wouldn't I remember dying?

Amy started to drift away. She looked so real to me that I thought of a play I had seen in which the actress was flying about, suspended by strings that I squinted to see, as the flying looked so real. Amy had no strings.

"She sent you to the garden," she replied to my question. She sighed, yet did not turn her face back to me. "She will stop at nothing, it seems," she added, as if confirming this notion for herself.

I wanted to cry out to her as she was fading. But other points that had been shimmering around us slowly formed orbs like miniature suns. And then the orbs throbbed and grew to become shapes of people. Ethereal figures of men, women, children, and infants in various clothes—obviously not those they were buried in. Bikers, horsemen, play clothes, gowns—I guessed to be the clothes that they loved best when alive, clothes that made them feel happy or confident. Clothes that stated how they wanted to be remembered.

Incredibly, I was not afraid. The spirits that surrounded me felt curious or kind, or paternal—these were the sentiments I was experiencing. Suddenly I could hear their thoughts—a cacophony of gentle pleas or scoldings seemingly directed at Amy. *She shouldn't be here, protect her, do something, Amy, somebody must.* I expected Amy to turn around and come back to me.

But instead I started falling and then my voice did come alive again as I screamed as I flailed against nothing until I crashed hard against a rough surface. I sat up, dazed initially, only to come to the shocking realization that I was in the back of a horse-drawn wagon, a blond wooden coffin decorated with black ribbons at my side. I looked around wildly for some clue as to where I was. But the wagon seemed to be the entire world as I strained to see around it. Nothing else seemed solid.

The wagon was covered with black streamers and ribbons, too. Now the coffin and I were bouncing against the hard wooden floor as two powerfully muscled horses, black ribbons trailing in the wind from their manes, pulled the wagon along at a dangerous clip. I could distinguish massive canopies of trees whirling about my head. It seemed to be dusk, and the trees that whirled past on both sides were blurring into one. Dirt from the roadway filled my nostrils. I squinted at the driver's seat as I realized that someone was holding the horses' reins. *It was Jenny who turned to smile deliriously at me.*

Jenny was dressed in a long black gown, and the black

veil that covered her head was parted to show her face. She dropped the reins and swirled her body around to jump into the thundering wagon beside me.

The noise from the horses' hooves and wagon was deafening. But despite that, Jenny's words were clear. "Get in," she commanded as I watched countless treetops flash over her head. "I want my daughter out."

She turned her back to me to start prying at the coffin with her fingers, she in her proper black and beaded gown, and her hair in a lovely chignon. Suddenly she seemed to grow to a monstrous size and strength as she threw open the coffin's lid. She then grabbed me by the waist with her black gloved hands to push me against it.

I looked down and screamed at the site of the freshly dead Amy looking sad and demure in a deep blue velvet dress with lacy white collars—a dress that must have been her mother's favorite.

"Get in!" Jenny screamed again, grabbing me by my hair this time to force me, headfirst to share the terrifying cramped space currently occupied by her daughter.

The wagon was careening back and forth. The very air seemed to be detonating, as if we were breaking the sound barrier. I pushed back with all of my might as Jenny continued to scream at me in fury.

"*Jessie, use your powers!*" I heard Paul cry through the chaos.

"*Amy, take control of your mother!*" commanded Elisha's stern voice.

Other voices swirled around me. I made out Marian's rallying cry to "Crush her!" Cindy's jaded advice to Amy in the coffin to make her mother "get real." And was it Eleanor or Claire, or both, who I could hear crying piteously, "This is not what we expected."

"You can't do this!" I screamed, pushing back now at Jenny with all of my strength, but Jenny possessed unearthly power. In seconds, my head was on her daughter's chest when she placed both gloved hands around my neck.

I heard a ringing, which vaguely pricked at my senses until I realized it was my cell phone. My mother! My own mother calling me to tell me to come home. I wanted to cry in defeat as I used my remaining strength to pry at Jenny's fingers. Instead I whimpered into Amy's chest, "My mother wants me to come home, Amy. Please help me."

Suddenly I was thrust backward, so hard that I fell against the unforgiving floor of the wagon. As I lay on my back in shock, I watched Amy spring up from her coffin to grab her mother's arms. I could barely make out Jenny's pale, beautiful face, now showing a mixture of surprise and pleasure. Her eyes flashed as her pleased smile caused her to look absolutely demonic. Amy look resigned.

"Why should I go with you, Mother?" Amy roared above the din. She was standing beside the coffin now, her long dark hair whipping about her face. She was gripping her mother's arms like a wrestler holds his opponent.

"Because I did it all for you!" Jenny screamed, her black mourning veil streaming behind her. Her knees were buckling as if they carried the weight of Amy's fury. "Could you not see that Thomas was using you?" Jenny's face twisted with fresh agony, as if her betrayal had happened only yesterday.

Amy's own face collapsed into bitterness. Her brown eyes gleamed with tears. She released her mother's arms, her own arms dropping lifelessly to her sides. "You really believe that, don't you?" she whispered, although the wind carried and amplified her words.

A smile tentatively crept onto Jenny's face. "It is true, my dear. You are my heart. I cannot move on till you are beside me." Jenny raised both her arms, beseeching Amy into her embrace.

My heart pounded as Amy turned her gaze toward me.

"You tell them that I am fulfilling my promise, that I have accepted my duty to remove a . . . disruptive spirit from the world." Her tears stopped. Her eyes took on a steely stare. "You tell Elisha that I *can* move on."

I nodded wordlessly as I watched Jenny's gloved hand cover her mouth in what appeared to be genuine surprise.

"Come along, Mother. You shall have your wish. Together we shall share eternity." Amy extended her hand.

"My precious daughter, you know I longed for this day," Jenny cried, as she grabbed her daughter's hand.

Amy's bitter laugh filled the air as the booming grew faint. She turned to me again. "Beware of your own mother. Keep those you love away from her."

And with that, she pulled her mother into the coffin and slammed the lid shut, sealing both of them in.

I felt paralyzed, as immobile as a statue, as the horses, both blacker than night, swiveled their thickly muscled necks as if to eyeball for themselves what all the commotion had been. Seeing only me, and the now mute coffin, they shook their heads and slowed to a canter and then a trot until finally they came to a stop, wheezing loudly through their flaring nostrils.

I edged away from the coffin, pressing my back against the wagon's side. Although the coffin appeared abandoned or lifeless, I swore I could sense an angry and desperate energy radiating from it. I felt a wave of heat roll over my body as the atmosphere began to quiver and thicken and blur as if I was being pushed underwater.

My cell phone rang again, and I found myself lying across the cool dirt of the graves as Paul, Elisha, and Adam knelt around me.

"Are you all right, girl?" Elisha asked as he poked at me with his mittened hand like I was a wild animal. His smile was proud.

Paul circled his arms around me, as if in a hug, but instead gently helped me into a sitting position. The smell of evergreens was sharp and caused my heart to race. His cool blue eyes stared into mine.

"You did it, Jessie. You accomplished a feat that none of us had been able to do. You convinced both spirits, mother and daughter, that they couldn't allow their pain and anger to destroy their larger community."

My cell phone finally stopped ringing. The relentless tone sounded sacrilegious here as I sat upon their graves.

Adam jumped up, surprisingly spry for an older man. "I want to gather the women to celebrate, especially that Marian." He gave us all an awful wink. "They just evaporated into the night with all of the excitement. You all wait here." And with that, he ambled past the black angel, squeezed between two sycamores, and disappeared into the dusky darkness.

This time I shook my head, to clear it of way too many impossible images that I knew would be burned into my brain for a lifetime. But right now, I just needed to know one thing, because my heart, despite everything that had happened tonight, felt heavy.

"Paul, Elisha, it did not end well for them," I stammered, the threat of tears welling behind my eyes. What was I crying for? Jenny and Amy, whom I only feared, or something greater than them? I think it was the idea that in the end, especially with death, everything had to be okay. "I thought we could make Jenny recognize how terribly she had hurt Amy, that she would truly seek Amy's forgiveness. And that Amy would forgive her and could actually love her mother again. Isn't that what we expected?" I cried.

"No, child," Elisha said with sympathy. "It's what you expected and it's also what made you strong. Hold on to that," he advised, taking my hand in his mittened one.

"Amy asked me to tell you that she could move on," I whispered. It was the least I could do for her.

Elisha nodded. "I knew she could."

"Jessie," Paul added softly. "I was like you. I thought

that the dead were wiser than the living. But I've learned that the spirits—we spirits," he emphasized, sweeping his hand to encompass the entire cemetery, "are not unlike living people. We can't make the spirits behave any better than their living selves. That's why they are still roaming the world."

"We haven't matured," Elisha said, a mischievous smile cutting into the side of his scruffy cheek. "None of us. Not even your handsome Paul here, although he's probably centuries ahead of most of us."

I needed to go home. I couldn't process anything here, among the spirits that tonight only confused and disappointed me. I struggled to stand. Paul and Elisha each grabbed me by an arm and pulled me to my feet.

"Miss Mary is waiting for you at the Entrance House. She will keep you company 'till your mother arrives," Paul said softly. "Later, we'll talk. I can help you understand. But I need you to know that tonight you were wonderful."

I nodded but couldn't offer a smile in return. I allowed Paul to guide me along the cobblestoned driveway, around the lightning-felled tree, to Miss Mary's comforting arms.

"Sleep tight," Elisha said. When I turned to look at him, he was gone.

Miss Mary and I were sitting on the bench outside of the Entrance House office as I waited for my mother. I had a glass of lemonade in my hands, which oddly enough made me feel almost normal. I noticed how the light of the moon outlined the stark forms of the geraniums in the pot beside us.

"You be sure to tell your mother that it was my fault, dear, keeping you in the back office to help with the invitations and flyers for our upcoming Tombstone Tea. I completely lost track of the time." Miss Mary tisked sweetly and shook her head at her absentmindedness.

The moon tinged Miss Mary's white hair with a soft aura. Her glasses looked so large on her tiny face and suddenly seemed the most solid part of her. A cool, gentle breeze caught her loosely fitting blouse.

"Thank you, Miss Mary," I replied, although I didn't really know what to say. How much did she know about this cemetery, about what went on here in the middle of the night? It was hard to tell, because in many ways she reminded me of a clueless grandmother.

Miss Mary pressed lightly against her hair. Marian had made the same gesture.

"You are a treasure to the cemetery, Jessie. Young

people like you who are willing to offer up your time."

I watched as the headlights of my mother's car lasered the darkness as she swung beneath the Entrance House arch, the lights catching tombstones and obelisks by surprise.

"Do you need a ride home, Miss Mary?" I asked.

"No, thank you, dear. My friend Elisha will be along at any moment," she said brightly.

She chuckled at my openmouthed response.

"Oh, silly me," she trilled. "I thought you knew that I am a spiritualist, just like you."

OUR
TOMBSTONE TEA

Epilogue

ays later, Paul told me that Jenny had sent me to the Garden—that place that provided the spirits a refuge from the living who insistently called out to them. He said this with his eyes and voice full of wonder. "As far as we know, no spiritualist has ever experienced this realm. This speaks to your gift, Jessie."

He must have seen the fear in my eyes, for he quickly added, "Do not worry. Our cemetery is peaceful now, thanks to you and Amy. You'll have time to develop your skills and gain confidence. I'll be here to help you."

His promise was like the sun slipping from a cloud to warm me all over.

At the moment, I was still carrying that warmth, that satisfaction that all was right as I watched Michelle check her reflection in the hand mirror that Jeanne held up to her face. Michelle was dressed as Margaret Fox, a famous spiritualist in the nineteenth century who, along with her sisters, was credited with starting Spiritualism. Elisha had married Margaret when he was a living nonbeliever in the movement, hoping to save her from the bad influences of her sisters. I marveled when I found this out—a side of Elisha that I could not fathom.

Michelle's blond hair was in a tight chignon, and she wore an ankle-length dress that billowed in the light spring breeze. She wasn't wearing her trademark eye shadow, and her lip gloss was light. She smiled at her reflection with satisfaction as she told us that she was truly aiming for authenticity. She then gave Jeanne a warning look to say, "No smart remarks." We were standing by Margaret Fox's obelisk, which was not far from the Halprins' final resting place.

I wanted to hug them both and Melanie, too, who was on the top of the cemetery ridge by the crypt of a *Titanic* survivor. I had just helped her drag up the hill the blow up raft that her father thought would add some levity to the event even though the *Titanic* had wooden boats. The girls, my new friends, who seemed in awe of me since my night in the cemetery last fall, were ready for Laurel Hill Cemetery's newly revived Tombstone Tea.

Together, we had recruited twenty-five other kids from school to help with the tea. I had assigned everyone a role from the research I had done under Miss Mary's guidance. This Tombstone Tea was going to be just like the one that Paul had pretended I was in the midst of last fall. Each student actor was assuming the persona and dress of the individual of the grave they stood by. Miss Mary was our director and I was her assistant. Miss Mary would also prepare the tea and scones that cemetery guests would be treated to after they completed their spirit circuit. Today was our last dress rehearsal and tonight was the first performance.

How incredibly life can change in the course of one year, I thought, as I watched a bunch of the kids fan out across the cemetery grounds in various dress, heading to their particular tombstone. In many ways, I felt like a completely different person. I wondered how many other people had the opportunity to experience the undeniable connection between the living and the dead. How many people really got to know history and the people that inhabited it?

My dad was astounded by the change in me. "I knew you would connect to your new school, Jessie, and make new friends," he said smugly. This was just two weeks ago, when he volunteered to drive me around to drop off Tombstone Tea flyers at libraries, schools, and recreation centers in the area. Mom helped me with the press release that Miss Mary sent to the newspapers, TV, and radio stations. So far we had sold fifty-six tickets for tonight's performance and nearly seventy for tomorrow's. Miss Mary thought part of our success was our advertising campaign. We used the original Tombstone Tea flyer to design our own, which I think gives the event a real eerie feel, as if one is stepping back in time. I didn't want to spoil it for her and tell her that kids my age love getting spooked. A cemetery at night is way better than a lame boardwalk haunted house.

I glanced back at the office to see Miss Mary standing by its front door. Her arms were crossed as she surveyed the activity before her. At my suggestion, the ticket money was going to be used to restore some of the cemetery's deteriorating monuments. She didn't seem a bit surprised and had bestowed on me one of her brightest smiles. Miss Mary knew. I was part of a special club.

I thought about Paul and wondered where he was at the moment. Sometimes I worried about how this would work being a normal person with friends and family while living this other life, too—with the dead. Miss Mary said it's a balancing act. That we find our way. That friendship and love transcend all boundaries. Paul just tells me not to worry about it now and when I see him, my worries dissolve.

For now, I plan to take my fellow spiritualists' advice and help my friends prepare for our Tombstone Tea. Paul told me he didn't want a preview. He and Elisha were saving themselves for our opening night. I will see them then. That is soon enough.

CASLON

WILLIAM CASLON (1693-1766) was one of the greatest English letter writers. He modeled his design after late 17th century Dutch type, integrating heavy strokes and thick, stubby serifs. Italic letters in Caslon have an uneven slope, and many versions do not include a bold weight.

The Caslon typeface was a favorite of English printers. It was used to set nearly every form of printed material from fine books to high-pressure advertising. Caslon's popularity later spread to America where it was used for the Declaration of Independence. In 1902 the staff of American Type Founders created Caslon 540, a typeface intended for use in advertising. Caslon typeface is still widely used today thanks to its legibility and aesthetic appeal.